Smiles

Mary Ellen Donat

Copyright 2021 Mary Ellen Donat
ISBN – 978-1-950613-66-3
Published by Taylor and Seale Publishing, LLC
2 Oceans West Boulevard
Unit 406
Daytona Beach Shores, FL 32118

Cover design and layout by Chris Holmes

Publisher's Note: This is a work of fiction. Names, characters, places, and incidents are a product of the author's imagination or used fictitiously. Locales and public names are sometimes used fictitiously for atmospheric purposes. With the exception of public figures or specific historical references, any resemblance to actual people, living or dead, or to businesses, companies, events, institutions, or locales is completely coincidental. Any historical personages or actual events depicted are completely fictionalized and used only for inspiration. Any opinions expressed are completely those of fictionalized characters and not a reflection of the views of public figures, author, or publisher.

Dedicated to

Tom Donat,

who has patiently listened to my stories for more than 50 years

and

Mimi and Bill Burch,

who keep the stories coming

Acknowledgements

I am grateful to everyone who fascinated and entertained by colorfully passing along oral family histories and lore:

My father, the late **Edward L. "Corky" Cordell**, whose last words to me is good advice: "Have fun!"

My mother, the late **Betty Peyton Cordell**. Her answer to an observation I once made that she was such a good cook because her mother probably sat in a rocker in their kitchen, instructing her as she worked: "Yes, and criticized everything I did."

My paternal grandmother, the late **Dorothy Martin Cordell**, who often told me, "You'd have loved my mother."

A favorite aunt, the late **Nadine (Peyton) Barth**, who with my mother during one afternoon of reminiscing, answered in unison when I asked if they had any happy childhood memories: "No."

A favorite aunt/cousin (don't ask) of my mother's, the late **Anna Benge**. I adored her and the stories she told about our "people" from the hills of Kentucky. Like my mother, I loved spending the night with her as a child.

The late **Dick Tiernan**, beloved Richmond, IN high school coach and athletic director whose memories and perspective enhanced my dad's stories. What a joy to see Dick coming, as a child and even more as an adult.

Tom Bartel, whose recollections and friendly encouragement are always a welcome boost.

Mary Dee Peyton, widow of my mother's brother, who can really tell a lively tale.

Special appreciation goes to others, most unnamed here, with generational stories of their own:

The late **Mildred Wooley Martin**, my paternal great-grandmother. Shortly before he passed away, my dad looked at me with clarity he'd not had for days and said, "I *love* you, Grandma."

Jeri Borchers and **Judy Jackson Scovronski**, whose grandparents befriended a sailor in Norfolk during WWII. Wouldn't Dad be so pleased to know we girls have maintained friendships forged as children in the scorching sand of Virginia Beach?

Agent **Donna Eastman** of Parkeast Literary Agency. She's always fair, supportive and encouraging. Plus, she graciously allowed me to adapt for this novel the memory of her father heroically saving a child from a fire.

Taylor & Seales editor **Veronica H. Hart** for her gentle leading in making this novel better than when she received it.

Sunday, June 20, 1937

He probably fell in love with her right then. Smiles had a soft spot for kids, underdogs, and the uncomfortably shy. He thought Theta Whittle pretty much fit all of those categories, sitting off to the side on a flimsy oak folding chair as if by sheer will she could blend into the clammy cement-block wall behind her. She held with careful firmness a faded Sunday school paperback like a Spanish fan. Only her eyelids, with their half-moons of short but thick lashes, could be seen above its tattered pages.

Her older brother casually leaned against the basement wall nearby, his arms folded across his chest with his own worn tract dangling from one athletic hand. He was, with calculated nonchalance, his youngest sister's guardian. Serious and quiet, Eddie Whittle was popular among students at Richmond, Indiana's historic Dennis Junior High School. Yet he didn't leave his protective post to join other freshmen, rowdy and carefree during this brief intermission between services in the upstairs sanctuary and Sunday school in the lower level's curtain-partitioned classrooms.

Smiles glanced at Eddie then returned attention to the girl as she lowered her book. He saw that she could have been pretty, with large dark eyes perfectly aligned above a knuckle of a nose. Her lips were thin, deeply colored. Smooth cheeks gave way to reticent dimples as she self-consciously bit her lower lip. But her auburn bangs were pulled severely off her uncommonly large forehead, secured with a naked bobby pin just to the side of a ragged part.

Smiles wondered why any girl would purposely make herself plain.

He saw Eddie shift his weight from one leg to the other, and with a bored sigh, squint over to the raucous boys, resting on Smiles' gaze. Too wholesome to be embarrassed, aware that Eddie had caught him staring at Theta, Smiles nodded a greeting. His open grin revealed a row of straight white teeth. His eyes, blue as a cloudless summer sky, projected a sincere welcome to the classmate new to his neighborhood church. Smiles crossed the room, absently shoving off a friend who'd stumbled into him while playing catch with a wadded hymnal page.

Theta knitted her brow at his approach, then quickly turned studied attention to her dog-eared tract.

Smiles

Chapter One

1924

His Story

Even before he could walk, they began to call him Smiles. It was a natural combination of his given name and unusually sunny disposition. *"He'll have advantages beyond the reach of my Irish heritage,"* his mother thought, which she perceived inferior to other immigrants from Great Britain. When quixotic Jacky Flaugherty married the usually stoic Porter Smythe, she drew upon American history's first love story and chose for their son the indisputably Anglican moniker Miles.

"I've quickly grown used to strangers' observations that Miles is the happiest baby they've ever seen. So, I always nod politely," Jacky acknowledged to friends with adept reservation what she already knew, simply allowing that her friendly son with the laughing eyes was a naturally good baby.

She was secretly pleased, though she credited not herself but her mother for endowing him with his bright temperament.

Shortly after Miles' birth in a squat three-room clapboard on a chilly September morning in 1922, Mildred Flaugherty had beamed with absolute devotion into the face of her first grandchild cradled in his mother's arms. Running a finger over the wispy blonde fuzz that constituted his hair, she softly advised her daughter, "Always smile at him, Jacky. If you smile at him, he'll be a smiler, too. And people who smile are naturally happy."

And so, when Jacky, barely awake at two in the morning, put the baby to her breast she smiled down on him as he looked into her eyes, cooing contentment. When she changed his damp and messy diapers, she smiled. She smiled when he pulled himself up from the kitchen floor by grasping the tablecloth, bringing dishes and the frosted glass condiment service down in a shower to spill and break on the unforgiving linoleum floor. Her smile softened her reprimand when he crawled too close to the wood stove or emptied lower cabinets to form around him a wreath of strewn cookware on her spotless floor.

She was smiling now, watching her toddler totter after his cousins in her mother-in-law's steep backyard, though her heart wasn't in it.

Porter's mother, Opal Smythe, could easily have been the inspiration for dark jokes with her sour, critical nature. She had nearly destroyed Jacky and Porter's marriage shortly after Smiles' birth when she talked her four sons into moving their families into her home near the railyards. She used as a weapon and a tool their father's debilitating stroke to assert her need for a tidy household of wage-earners and domestics, though she was careful not to use those terms in her curtly convincing case.

The men brought in good railroad wages. Each Friday they dutifully handed over crisp pay envelopes to their mother, still sealed. Their wives contributed free labor that included not only housekeeping but also caring for their invalid father-in-law.

Opal usurped her daughters-in-law's maternal privileges, liberally doling out her grandchildren's discipline without question or affection. She ruled her crowded home with despotic authority. Exceptionally small in stature but with mammoth supremacy, she dictated which daughter-in-law would watch the congress of children while the others cleaned or cooked. A kitchen chair, its back as wooden as her own, was dragged from room to room as she oversaw the daily changing of bed linens, early morning emptying and disinfecting of bedpans, and laundering and hanging out of sheets whatever the weather.

A severely tight topknot of greasy gray hair pulled back her stern black eyes into menacing slits as she supervised housecleaning along with thrice daily meal preparations. Her harsh expression changed little from setting to setting, reprimands frequent and encouragement delivered in the form of formidable silence.

"You're all right," a tearful Jacky was told by one of her sisters-in-law early in their residence. "If she didn't like the way you peeled them 'tatas, she'd have let you know it. The best compliment she cares ta give is sayin' nuthin.'"

But Opal was generous with switches broken from a nearby willow tree. She strictly wielded them herself against her grandchildren's skinny legs or bare bottoms. Crying by tots or toddlers was not tolerated, whether from injury or reprimand. And she was as proficient with her tongue as with the switch if a mother attempted to intervene or console her own child.

Jacky had quietly observed her mother-in-law's cruelty while cradling Miles in her arms, knowing his infancy could protect him for only a short time. Opal admonished her, "You're picking him up too soon when he cries. Don't rock him during the day, and in the evenings put him to bed promptly at seven. He don't need comfort of the gas light turned dim above his crib. It'll only serve to spoil the boy."

All of this Jacky bore with tight lips and heart until one early

November Saturday while Porter and his brothers worked the weekend day's half-shift.

Opal had sent her outside to hang sheets on the line. Jacky clutched wooden pins between her teeth and reached overhead to hang the wet muslin. When she came back into the kitchen, the empty bushel basket on her hip, Jacky saw her mother-in-law purposely giving Miles a sugar tit too close to the time he should have suckled at Jacky's breast. Miles was lying in the crook of the old woman's arm hungrily pulling at the wadded cloth.

Jacky dropped the empty basket, wrenched her son from Opal's grasp, and promptly marched out the front door without pausing to grab her wool jacket from its peg by the door. She also, in her haste, forgot Porter's rare hair-trigger temper. His possible violent reaction wouldn't have been a consideration for her in that moment anyway, since it was unlikely he'd been drinking so early in the day.

Jacky had carried her baby nearly four miles from northeast Richmond over the river gorge bridge to her own modest clapboard in the working-class neighborhood of Fairview. She fervently prayed all the way that Porter hadn't rented it out.

Jacky thanked her lucky stars to find the house empty. And then again as she pushed open the unlocked front door. Her warm wool coat wasn't the only thing she hadn't considered as she fled the Smythe family home. But then, her mother was only a block away; Jacky's childhood home was an unconventional option.

Despite the crisp autumn morning, Jacky had raised windows, first the front room, then the bedroom where Smiles had taken his first sweet breath, and finally the oblong kitchen situated behind both. Fresh air invaded and overcame months of stillness to ventilate the tiny rooms. She breathed deeply, inhaling liberty. She laughed as she exhaled.

Overjoyed to be in her own home again, she relished the prospect of scrubbing sheets and hanging them to dry in time to make up the bed where she would cuddle Miles as he slept beside her. Porter was not present in the imagined scene. Her only thought was for their cherubic son.

After pinning the last sheet to the wire strung from the house to the shed, she settled in a kitchen rocker to nurse Miles. That's where Porter found her.

Opal had dispatched an eight-year-old grandson to retrieve him from his Saturday morning trick at the railyard. She demanded, "Control your errant wife and bring her back in time for the girl to set the dinner table."

It would never have occurred to Porter to take Jacky's part against his mother. He'd hurried to Fairview with his only anxious thought being that he'd better return with her by noon or face wrath exceeding fury.

It was beyond Porter's imagination that the scene would play out any different as he flung open the back door of the modest Fairview house.

"Okay, Jacky," he said, closing the window above the kitchen sink, "you've given me enough trouble for the day. Finish up there while I close up the rest of the house. Where's the boy's diapers and whatnot?"

"I'm not a-goin' back," Jacky clipped through clenched teeth. "And if you try to take this baby out of this house, you'll have to come through me. And then I'll get my brothers to come take care of what's left of you."

Porter hadn't been sure what she meant by that, but had a frighteningly fair idea, and could clearly see that she meant it.

That night the three of them, Porter and Jacky with Miles

between them, kissed each other goodnight then drowsily, contentedly, fell asleep in their own home.

So now, these weekly Sunday dinners were all that remained of Opal's sway over the little family. Still, it galled Jacky that they joined the rest of the Smythe clan as helpless subjects to the demanding matriarch as serfs to a lord. Worst, one day out of every seven it was as if Smiles belonged to someone else. Someone who didn't agree with his other grandmother's erudite advice.

Seated on a wooden slat bench suspended with twisted ropes from the limb of a maple tree, Jacky, six months along with a second child, now watched as Smiles ran clumsily after his cousins toward hewn planks supported by sawhorses. The makeshift table was laden with early summer fruit Opal had requested for Sunday dinner. Jacky was horrified to see that someone had contributed an immature cantaloupe.

Watching her mother-in-law plunge a butcher knife into the pale green orb, she foresaw trouble. "Don't give Smiles any of that muskmelon! You know he's but one and a half," she called.

Opal narrowed her eyes, conjuring a challenge. Her grandchildren at that moment came tumbling one after another, stopping short of the makeshift table. The crone bent at the waist, giving Smiles something hidden by her billowing black skirt. Jacky bolted from the swing to intercept what she instinctively knew was the unripe fruit.

Before she could reach him, Smiles turned. Jacky was appalled to see a trail of juice staining the front of his cotton dress. His chin was sticky with it. Catching him up, she turned on her mother-in-law who was coolly presiding over the cutting of a honeydew.

"I told you not to give this baby muskmelon."

"It won't hurt him," Opal returned.

Jacky, whose mother had many times warned of the danger of feeding melon to babies, could see that the damage was already done, though the child was laughing and nuzzling her cheek.

She said again, more forcefully, "I *told* you not to give this baby muskmelon. If he gets sick, you're to blame."

It could have been a coincidence but Jacky would never believe it. Tight screams awakened her before midnight in the Fairview house. Jacky rushed to Miles' crib. She put her hand to his forehead knowing before she touched him that it would be hot and dry. He stilled briefly then drew a short breath that he held long seconds until it exploded into a wail. Not a demanding cry, but one she recognized as a baby's expression of pain. His quivering legs were tight against his abdomen. Pulling his nightshirt away from his extended stomach with both chubby fists, he tossed his head side to side.

Jacky carried him to the kitchen where she dampened a dishcloth and held it to his forehead, alarmed by how quickly its soggy coolness heated. Calling to Porter, she laid Miles in the galvanized sink and pumped cool water into the bath. Her darling son screamed and she realized that the stream must feel like ice against his burning flesh. Through painful wails he beseeched her with pleading and confused eyes.

"I know," Jacky tried to sooth. "I'm sorry, my baby. But we've got to get this fever down."

Porter stumbled into the kitchen, rubbing a palm across his right eye. He came to the sink and took the dishcloth from Jacky's hand.

"I'll do this," he said, swiping the now lukewarm water over Miles' head and back. "You go get the Kepler's."

Jacky rushed to the ice box for the cod liver oil. She grabbed a soup spoon from the drawer and spilled more than she poured. "I'm shaking so bad . . ."

"Here," Porter said, leaving the torturous bathing. "I'll give it to him."

Miles saw the familiar Kepler's carton and tried to hold shut his mouth but couldn't long contain his cries. Porter, wincing, tilted a spoonful of the slimy cod liver oil into Miles' mouth, so wide with screaming that he could see the child's tonsils. Miles gurgled and swallowed, held his breath, and yowled. He grasped in turn his mother's nightdress and his father's muscled bicep, unable to find comfort.

Porter again took over the dishcloth bathing as Jacky attempted to comfort her son, gently rubbing his stomach with her middle and index fingers while cooing into his ear. At last his temperature began to decrease, but the baby's torment seemed to intensify. Miles struggled to get out of the sink and into his mother's arms. Porter stood his son in the bath and pulled the sopping nightshirt over the child's head. He dried him with a dish towel, wrapped him in it, and motioned for Jacky to go sit in the rocker by the stove.

She rocked only a few moments, Smiles lifting himself from her lap, arching his back and pulling at the towel covering his stomach. Jacky continued to speak softly to him but was undone. "I've got to get him to Mom."

"I'll get your robe," Porter said, already heading to the bedroom. When he returned, the rocker was empty and the kitchen door was open to the night.

Jacky stumbled over cracked sidewalks illuminated only by a waning moon moving in and out of ominous clouds. Porter caught up with her but she refused to give up her wailing child. He trotted beside them the three blocks to the Flaugherty's, trying in vain to cradle Miles' head as Jacky ran. He then hurried ahead to pound on his in-laws' door. The porch light came on and the door opened just as Jacky reached the front walk.

Mildred, in her nightdress, took the writhing child from his mother's arms, shushing him with kisses as he bellowed his agony. Jacky followed them into the front room, tearfully caressing Smiles' forehead.

Angry words tumbled through her fear. "That old woman gave him muskmelon, Mom! I told her not to, but of course she did anyway. Now look at our sweetheart. What's going to happen?"

Mildred laid Miles on the front room davenport. Streams of tears ran into his ears as he tossed his head from side to side. His screams punctuated his grandmother's soft probing of his abdomen, her brow reflecting a testament to the worry rising from her own stomach to her breast. "I don't know," she said, wiping her own warm tears from the boy's naked torso.

Mildred took Miles from the davenport and held him securely close to her bosom with a constricting embrace. She carried him to a rocking chair, its horsehair well-worn. "Git the quilt from my bed, Jacky, and tuck it snug over the both of us. Real tight."

In his grandmother's practiced arms, Miles slept fitfully, awakened by sharp pains every quarter hour. Jacky anxiously counted the mantel clock's lazy chimes each hour throughout the rest of the night. Finally eight notes sounded with excruciating precision and the doctor was at last summoned.

After examining Miles on the dining room table, pressing cold fingers into his groin, causing the toddler to renew hoarse cries, Dr. Misner turned grim eyes to Mildred and Jacky.

"This baby is gravely ill. Give him nothing but warm rice water. It's important that you strain all grain from the broth. Do you understand? Give him only water that the rice has been boiled in. His little intestines couldn't stand anything more."

Taking another look at his young patient, Dr. Misner patted Jacky's shoulder. "We won't lose him; just as long as you follow my instructions. It'll be a long haul, but the little fella should make it all right."

If not for her terror, denying Miles filling sustenance would have been the worst consequence for Jacky. The first week following Dr. Misner's stern warning, the baby cried incessantly for solid food and fatty milk. She felt the weighted tug of yearning at his wails but resisted, heartbroken that he couldn't understand her denial. Reluctantly, she permanently relinquished her son to her own mother, for she couldn't bear to hold him as he cried hungry tears.

She'd loved nursing him, singing as she rocked, watching him nuzzle her breast, running his soft hand over it, gently pressing her sweet milk into his sighing mouth. The memory was raw as Jacky desolately watched as her mother held her baby, cooing to him as he urgently pulled at the nipple of the bottle that held nothing more than thin, cloudy rice water.

Over the next two months, her cherubic boy became thinner and thinner until his sallow skin hung loose over sharp bones. He no longer toddled as he grew weak from malnutrition. By the time Sis was born two weeks before his second birthday, Miles barely turned in his crib. His languid eyes lacked focus and he no longer laughed. Neither did he cry.

His only complaint, as Mildred pushed the rubber nipple into his mouth, was to faintly beg as he remembered the food behind the taint. "Ri'e, Mom. Ri'e."

Chapter Two

1926

His Story

It seemed Smiles couldn't get enough tapioca. He craved its flavor of sweet rice, relished the way it filled then squished voluminously in his mouth, ladled by the tablespoon until his cheeks bulged. He was surrounded by bowls and bowls of it. Laughing, he dipped the gigantic spoons grasped in both fists into multiplying bowls and shoveled warm tapioca into his mouth with the speed of a fire horse. Oh, it was so good!

The aroma of tapioca simmering on the stove invaded Smiles' saccharine dream bringing him to consciousness. He knew Mom would be standing over it, a hand to her hip, patiently stirring as the pudding slowly thickened. Smiles and Sis were lying feet-to-feet on their grandmother's narrow davenport. The overstuffed pew had been their cot in the Flaugherty's front room as Jacky was confined in her parents' back bedroom following the birth of their baby sister the week before.

Careful to not disturb Sis, Smiles slipped from the sofa and padded softly to the kitchen. "Mom," he whispered hopefully, tugging his grandmother's skirt, "is it ready?"

"Just in time," Mildred said, turning a ready and unreserved smile to her grandson. "Git me a deesh. Hush now, so you don't wake up your sisters."

Shaking his sandy Dutch boy seriously as he handed her a small Willow bowl, Smiles assured, "Oh, no, I'm quiet, Mom. Just give me a little so there'll be lots of tackioca lef' for Sis an' Precious."

Mildred laughed, covering her mouth to contain the delight that regularly overflowed for her grandson. She knew the

11

saucepan should be bubbling with rolled oats or Baby Rastus' cream of wheat. But she liked the pleasure that tickled her breast with love and joy as she placed the bowl steaming with warm tapioca before her cherished grandson. He'd been deprived for too long to make him wish and want when she blessedly had it within her control to please him with anything he cared to unreservedly devour.

"There's plenty for ever'body," she beamed, "but I think you'd better eat Presh's share. My, how you're a-fillin' out. You're going to be as big as Santy Claus!"

"Oh, I like Santy Claus." Smiles laughed, climbing onto a kitchen chair. "I'm going to be Santy Claus' helper when I grow up. Cause I gots a big belly an' 'cause I can help him make kids happy."

His cheeks chubby with spoonsful of pudding, Smiles gulped to swallow. Want had beckoned and nurtured a new habit of wolfing meals like a competitive puppy at a communal plate. With eager eyes he beckoned his grandmother to listen even though his words were thick with creamy tapioca. "My man wants me to make kids happy, Mom."

Mildred had heard this before. At first, she thought it was a dream he'd had when he was near to death, but now she wasn't so sure. He was too earnest, and too often brought up the visit he had when he was so weak he could barely open his eyes. He frequently described in confident detail the giant man and his kind eyes, radiantly blue.

When Smiles was able to sit up following the months of bedrest, Jacky had brought him paper and crayons to entertain him the long hours he was to be kept quiet. At first, they were just toddler's scribbles. He'd point to the drawing, earnestly explaining its meaning. "My man!"

But as the months and years passed, he perfected the image

that so fascinated him. Dozens upon dozens of progressively skillful drawings depicted a colossal man dressed in a flowing robe sitting beside a child's bed. His bed.

"We're s'posed to love one 'nother," he said seriously whenever he relayed conversations he'd had with the mysterious sickbed caller. And then he continued as if the realms of imagination and reality were one. He did so now.

"That's the most 'portant thing and easy if we love Jesus first. Can I have more, Mom? Is there 'nough?"

Mildred took up his dish and turned to carry it to the simmering pot on the cookstove. She leaned over to kiss Smiles' mussed hair. "I love you a bushel and a peck."

Smiles tugged at the muslin apron safety-pinned at its edges to her blouse, drawing her down to eye level. Wrapping plump arms around her collar, he finished, "And a hug around the neck!"

Chapter Three

1926

Her Story

While four-year-old Smiles was feasting on bowls of tapioca in his grandmother's toasty Fairview home, three-year-old Eddie Whittle was laboriously chewing an uneven piece of days-old bread. It was spread thick with speckled bacon grease.

Three children shivered as they quietly munched the tough slices of stale bread. The sparse kitchen was not yet warmed by the spring sun. The cookstove was cold, the small stack of wood piled beside it untouched as older children by their mother's first husband had again hurried off to school without breakfast or lunch pails. Eddie pulled his sweater closed, wishing he hadn't lost the last button.

He, his older sister Camille, and younger sister Marlene were sitting cross-legged on straight-back chairs, their shoulders hunched to ward off the chill. The girls were huddled under a tattered quilt and Camille opened it in silent invitation to Eddie. Seeing the gooseflesh on her chalky bare legs, Eddie shook his head. The three chewed their scant breakfast, slowly savoring the bacon's flavor preserved in the salvaged lard. Like Smiles, they were being quiet so they wouldn't wake a baby.

No longer the youngest at three months shy of two years old, Marlene studied her brother and sister and attempted to mimic them. She was well aware that she was one of them now. However reluctant, she was a big sister. Eddie, born just eleven months after four-year-old Camille, assumed leadership of the siblings. It was he who'd taken the unsliced loaf of Honey Boy from the dented tin bread box and pulled a chair to the stove to retrieve the can of drippings. He carefully cut thick hunks of bread to place on the bare table before his sisters, taking the hard, crusty heel himself. The three wordlessly chewed, their dark eyes too serious for ones so young. Eddie licked at the lard on his bread and then playfully stuck out his tongue at sullen Marlene. They were, after all, too young to fully realize the truth of their straits.

Camille's birth had been joyous. Though she was her mother's eighth child, she was her father's first. Eddie, coming along so soon after his sister, was nevertheless welcomed with celebration. A boy. Another first for their proud, cigar-puffing father who insisted on naming his son after Eddie Ambrose, a favorite jockey.

Marlene's birth was somewhat less happily anticipated. But when she arrived, her father immediately fell in love with this new baby. While Camille and Eddie favored their mother's people, the Kents, along with their Cook half-siblings from May Nelle's first marriage, this wiry baby with the dimpled chin resembled her father.

Then May Nelle had become pregnant again.

Mr. Whittle, as the latest arrival would always refer to the four youngest children's father, didn't have a chance to overcome the disappointment that acquired love for her would surely have eased. He'd succumbed to pneumonia three months before her March-lion birth. Theta was destined to remain the resented eleventh child in a fatherless house that could barely feed ten.

The oldest of May Nelle's children were nearly adults, practically through high school. All seven Cook kids, including ones barely out of knickers, worked menial jobs to pump life into the blended family's perpetually hemorrhaging coffer like hopeless transfusions. Even with the gulf of age and paternity between them, May Nelle's combined offspring didn't consider each other half-brothers or -sisters. Every one of them was singly and corporately bound to the mother as with a corded rope of three strands representing Mother/Cooks/Whittles.

Together, they were whole with no possibility or desire of separation from their mother or each other. Together they were unbreakable.

But now the strongest thread was fraying as she lay beneath carefully mended heirloom quilts, debilitated by grief and worry.

May Nelle couldn't bring herself to turn red-rimmed eyes to the baby lying quietly in a worn crib beside her bed. As yet unaware of her undesirable status, Theta was already demonstrating the curiosity that would be her saving grace. Studying the colorful floral pattern of the stained wallpaper, her round sable eyes blinked quizzical concentration. She cooed fascination. It would have been an endearing sound to the woman lying in the bed if she hadn't been preoccupied with figuring how much longer they could stay in this house before eviction.

"Even with the seven older children contributing, I've not enough to pay the full rent again this month," she mumbled.

May Nelle turned her head into her pillow. Theta's song was merely a subliminal lullaby against thoughts of her first babies, now her sources of survival. The oldest two children had been named after the first two books of the New Testament. Then she'd gotten mixed up and named the next one John. Luke came next and finally a daughter, Ruth. Barely four months after Peter's birth, May Nelle had found herself pregnant again.

She'd proclaimed, "This seventh child will be my last." To put an exclamatory halt to her procreating, she named the girl May Belle, which always, to the girl's undying consternation, came out "Mabel."

From recollections of those older children's births, May

Nelle's thoughts suddenly segued to death. She glanced at Theta, whose coos were proof that she was unaware of the knot of worry she roused in her mother's bosom. May Nelle swallowed panic as her heart was once again pierced by fright.

She muttered to herself, "It was folly to buy the Earlham Cemetery plot. I wish I hadn't depleted our sparse sugar bowl bank account to bury Wendel with such extravagance. But I'm not sorry. I owed him too much to allow him to lie in a pauper's grave without a proper laying out.

"It was a miracle that he married me, a widow with seven children. Of course, when we met, he didn't know I'd been married before."

He was also unaware that six children were safeguarded in Lexington's Methodist Children's Home and another, the youngest boy, was all but adopted by a paternal aunt.

Newly widowed, May Nelle Cook had been desperate to recover her seven children, had resolutely refused adoption considerations, even though a farmer had wanted Matthew and Mark. She was sick at stomach and heart every time she thought of her Catholic sister-in-law gaining guardianship of her impressionable Peter.

She'd had no idea how she would ever get them all back but she knew she would, and when that day came, she'd see that they all came home. Every one.

She reflected on her miracle.

Wendel Whittle was a resident of the Louisville boarding house where May Nelle had taken work cooking and cleaning in exchange for her room and board, plus a dollar a week. Once, while leaning over to serve a boarder across from him, she'd caught Wendel's eye then quickly cast hers downward; not to the platter in her hand but to the bursting third button of her shirtwaist.

The button predictably intrigued Wendel Whittle.

After that, he now and again caught Miss Cook watching him from the corner of her eye. He thought she was lovely as she turned away, pressing her lips in a pleased smile. Bending with back straight to serve another boarder, she would glance at him then quickly turn her eyes downward. His eyes naturally followed.

It wasn't long before he determined to bring her out of this perceived shyness so that he might see if her teeth were intact or riddled with decay. Even a thoroughbred could be misjudged from a distance. He'd always taken closer looks before making a Derby choice. More than once he'd called off bets before his initial choice entered the gate. This was his policy on or off the track, whether fillies or females.

By the time he convinced May Nelle to openly smile and saw that she was not only still in possession of all her teeth, but that they were also gleaming though slightly crooked and overlapping, he began to fancy her. He liked the way she ironed his shirts and the way her dark eyes brightened when he gave her an extra penny for her fine work.

Wendel was a barber. He appreciated that her hair was always clean and brilliant no matter the season. What piqued and held his interest most, though, was that hers wasn't the waiflike figure of most housemaids but was seductively Rubenesque.

May Nelle wasn't blind to Mr. Whittle's interest. Despite his being nearly two decades her senior, she was taking note herself. Of the way he promptly paid his rent, the high polish of his unscuffed shoes, the number of suits in his closet (three). And then there was his grammar and dialect. She began to categorize boarders by their dinner table conversations. Mr. Whittle without fail exhibited impeccable speech with a pleasing drawl rather than a twang.

May Nelle knew Wendel noticed that she gave him the gizzards when Sunday chicken was served, surely aware that her breasts grazed his back as she leaned over his shoulder. His bed linens were crisp and smooth, unscarred by multiple mendings as other boarders' were. Her fingers innocently lingered against his as she returned an ironed shirt, one whose missing button had been replaced without his mentioning it.

One day, he opened the door to his room to find her bending deeply over from the waist to dust the floor beneath the bureau directly opposite.

"Miz Cook," he said that evening following supper, "would you care to join me for a stroll to Woolworth's for a phosphate?"

They kept company the remainder of the summer, enjoying walks while the sun burned amber on the horizon, or taking in evening air on the boarding house veranda. Sometimes Mr. Whittle carried chairs from the kitchen through the mud porch onto the back lawn where they could chat in privacy under the drooping branches of a black cherry tree. There, he regaled her with tales of his trips to horse races at Churchill Downs or as far away as New York's Aqueduct. It was, May Nelle quickly learned, his favorite pastime.

That was another thing she knew he liked: She listened.

By the time he learned about the untimely death of a first husband, and the existence of seven children, May Nelle believed he was already smitten. He'd not been thinking of those children the fall evening he asked her to marry him. Hadn't considered that they'd be a part of this new marriage until May Nelle began to speak of their return as if it were expected. She had so beguiled him that he thought he would do anything to at last share her bed.

She displayed a full set of healthy teeth the night he said that if she would agree to marry him the next week, he would take in her seven children. She treated him to those pearly whites again the day he rented a two-story home with three bedrooms on Louisville's near south side.

He'd guessed correctly that her grin was an expression of intense love but had misjudged the direction of that devotion.

Tears streaming at the thought of the dear price of Mr. Whittle's grave in Earlham Cemetery, May Nelle wasn't rethinking that decision as she watched with detachment as little Theta put the toes of her right foot into her hungry mouth. Even if he hadn't rescued six of her children from the orphanage, and wrested Peter from the boy's Catholic aunt, May Nelle wouldn't have let him be buried in an ignominious manner. She was indebted to him not only because he'd restored her family, but also because she'd been a young widow with a life sentence of hard labor in someone else's kitchen. Despite her large ready-made family, he'd saved her.

Still, there was this month's rent.

Theta's coos turned to demanding cries. Reluctantly, May Nelle rose and gathered up the warm bundle. She returned to bed and propped herself on pillows, undid her nightdress and drew out a bloated breast. As the child took ferocious hold, May Nelle smoothed the dusky curls on the satin head. It was a gesture of rote without fondness. Theta tugged at the breast as if sucking the life from her. May Nelle closed her eyes against the sight of this greedy burden.

Knowing the other Whittle children would be able to hear her, May Nelle stifled her despair with a balled fist. Even though her breasts heaved with sobs, the baby was oblivious to the anxiety that lay beneath. *Why*, May Nelle thought angrily, *am I saddled with this child?*

"How will I ever get through this?" she moaned aloud.

And then she knew. Though she'd thought more than twice before that each of her most recent female deliveries would be her last, she'd never entertained the popular notion that any of them would be carefully groomed to be her comfort in old age.

Now, for the first time, she did.

Chapter Four

1932

Her Story

Theta held her mother's hand instead of the other way around, as they boarded the Greyhound in Richmond. They were headed to her Aunt Shirlee Kent's in the hills of Jefferson County, Kentucky. It threatened rather than promised to be a long day. They left before dawn and stopped to change buses in Indianapolis before heading south to Louisville where they would deliver Theta's sisters Camille and Marlene to Ruth and May Belle. Then, mother and youngest daughter would board a local bus that would at last drop them at the foot of Aunt Shirlee's quarter-mile washboard lane.

The three little girls had been too sleepy before leaving home to eat the stale biscuits their mother had spread with apple butter. Though May Nelle had wrapped the meager breakfast in waxed paper to eat as they traveled U.S. 40 to the state capitol, it'd been decided to leave the crumbling sandwiches for their brother Eddie. They liked the thought of sacrificing for him, who would be spending the summer with their brother John in order to play baseball. It'd been a singular honor for Eddie to be asked to man first base on an older-boys' Legion team.

The bus jostled and jolted along the Old National Road, stopping in every burg and ville along the way to pick up or deposit passengers. May Nelle rested her head against the cracked plastic seat back, her eyes closed. Theta sat next to her, by the window. It was fascinating to see the light from the rising sun push against the rear of the bus then gradually creep up brick buildings as they proceeded west. Theta strained forward, tilting her head past her mother's rising and falling chest, to see if her sisters were witnessing the same phenomenon across the aisle, but they were propped against one another, apparently asleep.

Theta had long tired of the looping scenery of two-story brick storefronts, fields, clapboard farmhouses then brick storefronts again and again by the time they reached the outskirts of Indianapolis. Homes and businesses on the edge of the big city differed little from those in her own small town, but as the bus labored toward the Greyhound terminal near the city's Circle, buildings grew and morphed into limestone fortresses.

Though May Belle and the other girls had slept through the frequent stops during the interminable journey, they startled awake when the bus pulled to a final, jolting stop in Indianapolis. May Nelle groaned as she maneuvered her girth through the crowded space between her seat and the one in front, stepping awkwardly into the narrow aisle. Though her pocketbook straps were laced over her arm, she cradled the bulky cloth purse to her chest.

"Don't ferget yer bags, girls," she warned, not looking back as she careened like a drunken sailor toward the front exit.

Camille then Marlene then Theta followed behind, each clutching a carefully folded brown paper sack wrinkled with reuse from Shorty's corner grocery. Inside, along with some personal treasures such as toilet water in Marlene's case and books as in Theta's, were a change of underwear and a home-sewn dress. Each girl routinely wore one set while the other was washed and hung to dry. It had, as yet never occurred to any of them that there was need for more than two garments in their wardrobes.

The night before, Marlene had huffed as she'd packed Camille's hand-me-downs in her sack. In the downstairs bedroom she shared with her mother, Theta had said aloud as she rolled a dress to place in her bag, "I'm glad that Camille and

Marlene wore all the stiffness out of my clothes. They're so much more comfortable now."

In the waking Indianapolis terminal, May Nelle sat heavily on a hard oak deacon's bench, one of dozens lined up in the center of the cavernous waiting room. She pulled three wax paper triangles from her purse. She offered two of the packages to Camille and Marlene, along with an apple each.

"Might as well have it now." May Nelle sighed.

The two sisters devoured the shrunken apples and peanut butter sandwich halves that May Nelle had meant for lunch. She'd underestimated not only the length of the sixty-mile trip from Richmond to Indianapolis, but also her daughters' hunger. The snacks were a rare treat May Nelle had planned as a surprise for her daughters during the long journey from Indianapolis to Louisville.

The girls had never tasted Peter Pan though Marlene had many times complained that she was the only one in her class who hadn't. It was with this in mind that her mother had washed and pressed two dozen choir robes for First English Lutheran Church to earn enough extra money to buy a jar.

From the corner of her eye Theta watched her sisters bite into their sandwiches then tipped her chin, pretending to admire the frosted glass chandeliers hanging from the pressed tin ceiling. She brushed invisible dirt from the bench then purposely appeared content to quietly sit next to her mother as if still mesmerized by the light fixtures.

May Nelle opened the remaining wax paper triangle, tore the half-sandwich in two, and handed a ragged piece to Theta. She'd meant to make two sandwiches, but after sawing the last of the Honey Boy loaf thicker than she planned, she only had slices enough for a sandwich and a half.

"Now you won't have nothing left to eat on the bus," she

admonished, reluctantly giving up the last apple to her youngest daughter.

"Don't care," Camille said, thinking the rebuke was meant for all three girls. "We were hungry. And I like this new peanut butter!"

"I like the kind with the itty-bitty peanuts in it better," Marlene said, though she'd never tasted the spread before.

Camille reached for the scalloped crusts Marlene had left uneaten in her crumpled waxed paper. "I'll eat the rest of yours."

Theta nibbled the quarter-sandwich from the half she and May Nelle shared. "I'm so full," she said, slowly chewing to make the piece last longer. "I'm glad I didn't have to eat a whole one. And I like the way we cut the sandwiches diagonal, Mom."

She emphasized the plural pronoun closely linking her with their mother, as if it were a particular privilege.

Since she also shared a bed with their mother, she'd been awakened earlier than her sisters that predawn morning and had helped make their lunches by the dim light of a single bulb hanging above the kitchen table. She had cut the sandwiches, remembering the picture from her mother's *Modern Screen* magazine showing Irene Dunne presenting a plate of fancy sandwiches to her unseen guests.

Theta hadn't dared waste the day-old Honey Boy by cutting off the crusts, and they didn't have olives or fancy toothpicks to top the triangles, but she was sure she'd achieved somewhat the same effect. Watching Marlene snatch the remaining bits of crust from Camille's groping fingers in the bus station, she felt a satisfaction that exceeded her pride.

May Nelle had been right. The girls were famished by the time they reached Louisville in late afternoon. Ruth and May Belle, the Whittle girls' Cook half-sisters, met them at the crowded station, standing outside waving embroidered hankies as the Greyhound lumbered onto the Louisville lot.

"Hello! Hello!" they chorused.

The Cook sisters, May Belle barely out of her teens, had gotten work in the Kentucky metropolis and lived together in a shotgun walk-up above a corner grocery in the East Market District. It'd become an annual ritual for them to take Camille and Marlene, their Whittle half-sisters, for the summer. It wouldn't be thought of, by either of them, to also invite Theta. At seven, the little girl was her mother's resigned companion.

After a brief reunion, just long enough for May Nelle to lightly kiss each of her older daughters on powdered cheeks, Ruth and May Belle turned away to guide their charges from the parking lot. They'd scarcely noticed the youngest Whittle, silently standing in the shadow of their mother.

Theta watched her two closest sisters round the corner of the terminal skipping hand in hand with other sisters she barely knew. She caught a glimpse of May Belle handing Marlene what looked to be a Baby Ruth. It was quickly becoming America's favorite candy bar. A pang of envy wrestled with rising hunger, but she didn't allow either to surface.

Instead, she picked up the paper sack that constituted the mother and daughter's combined suitcase and led May Nelle to a scarred bench leaning haphazardly alongside the building. Stomach audibly growling, Theta hoped they wouldn't have to wait long for the connecting bus that would wind around hilly switchbacks toward the tiny hamlet of Rabbit Hash.

The small local Greyhound deposited them at the bottom of a steep hillside overlooking the cleavage of other, lower hills. The distant Ohio River, separating Kentucky from Indiana, was invisible from where they stood. Dense branches hanging over the dusty road blocked the setting sun. Theta knew the way to Aunt Shirlee's from here, so she impatiently grasped her mother's hand to hurry her to the narrow dirt lane halfway up the ridge before darkness fully set in.

She hungrily hoped that Uncle Honey had killed a chicken.

Soon, Theta could see smoke rising from her kin's stone chimney against the purple dusk. She wanted to run toward it, but her desire was thwarted by the tightening grasp of her mother's hand. May Nelle gasped for air, panting as she relied on her tiny daughter to pull her forward.

They waited supper! Theta grinned for the first time that day; for the first time in what seemed like months. She loved Aunt Shirlee and Uncle Honey. In reality her first cousins, her mother's niece or nephew – she wasn't sure which of them was actual relation – the pair was closer in age to her mother. Summering with them and their brood in the blue hills of Kentucky was mere consolation for Camille and Marlene's prize. But hurrying toward the welcome curl of wood smoke, Theta at this moment felt she honestly didn't care.

She was anxious to show Aunt Shirlee how she'd learned to press flat pieces like tablecloths and handkerchiefs as she worked alongside her mother over the past winter. She might, if given the opening, brag that it'd been she who discovered that adding one part of water to two parts Oswego starch would stretch the product without diminishing its effect. But she'd die before she'd embarrass May Nelle by mentioning that when her mother's customers picked up their clean and pressed laundry she never expected praise for her part in the washing and ironing. From either the customers or her mother.

As the ramshackle cabin, with additions clearly distinguished by varying stages of weathering, came fully into sight, Theta adopted a smug attitude. She wouldn't want to be in that sultry, noisy city with her sisters when she could sit with Aunt Shirlee and Uncle Honey on their slanting front porch, enjoying the cool night breeze that seemed to drift toward stars so close she could almost reach out and capture them like fireflies.

Her sisters might have eaten cafe hamburgers, but she was sure to get chicken n' dumplin's and a fat slice of Aunt Shirlee's rhubarb pie. Later, her sisters might gaze at Errol Flynn on a theater screen, but she'd be admiring the Big Dipper, lying on her back on a cushion of thick, fragrant bluegrass.

Her stars, she told herself and anyone who asked, were superior in every way.

"Hurry, Mom; they're waiting for us!"

Shirlee and Honey rocked woodenly in straight-back kitchen chairs, the front legs rhythmically pounding the porch floorboards with teetering of the chairs' back legs. Shirlee held a baby. Theta knew from experience that the rain barrel beside the cabin was filled with the infant's soiled diapers. And probably little Josephine's, too. She could see the toddler digging in the dirt in front of the porch with an ornate serving spoon. Older children danced in the yard like nymphs as they pursued twinkling lightning bugs.

Aunt Shirlee shifted the baby to her husband's arms and rose to joyfully welcome their visitors. Theta wanted to rush to encircle Aunt Shirlee's waist with skinny arms, her glee easily lifting her from the yard to the porch, but she didn't dare pull away from her mother's clutch. It would be perceived as disrespect. Instead, Theta shyly smiled with the reticence her mother expected. It was with willpower born of fear that Theta waited to embrace Aunt Shirlee, and to at last see what was simmering in that black cast iron pot over glowing embers just inside the door.

After a meal of butter beans smothered with new green onions and vine ripened tomatoes, Theta lay behind the shed with a number of her second cousins. Both stomach and spirit full, she breathed deep the freedom that filled her bosom only in this beautiful place.

"Look," she said, pointing out various constellations, patiently instructing her rapt audience in the tone and voice of her first-grade teacher. "Orion is standing next to the river Eridanus with his two hunting dogs, Canis Major and Canis Minor. They're fighting Taurus the bull. See there?"

"You know just about ever'thin', Theta," Junior said with wonder.

Theta glanced sideways at her cousin, Shirlee and Honey's oldest boy, who lay beside her. She could barely contain a pleased smile as she accepted the rare compliment as if she expected it, though she suppressed ecstatic rapture with lips pressed tight. Lying in the cushiony grass, she began to feel rich instead of scared.

The Christmas before, when she unwrapped her only present, a square of an old blanket hemmed with rainbow embroidery thread, she suddenly realized just how poor they really were. Each Whittle girl had received a doll blanket but no doll. From that sparse holiday on, she began to worry about their meager larder and if – no, *when* they'd be forced to move to yet another furnished house. Moving to a smaller, lesser rental also meant moving to a new school with a classroom of students who were strangers only to her.

Each day the past six months, her stomach muscles had progressively clenched tighter and tighter with involuntary anxiety. Now, at last home in the familiar Kentucky hills among children who believed she was the embodiment of big-city sophistication, Theta sighed contentment.

From the moment Aunt Shirlee's worn but stable house had come into view this evening, she'd begun to relax. In these embracing hills, she was safe. In this home, she was a child among children. Best, during summers with the Kents, she was exceptional as her mother's only child instead of the unhappy tail end of nearly a dozen.

Theta reveled in the knowledge that her curiosity and intelligence were admired here. The dull evenings she'd spent reading quietly beside her mother while her sisters played dress-up in another room had been amply rewarded by Junior's simple words of approval.

"Does Eddie like lookin' at the stars, too?" he asked.

Theta smiled, thinking fondly of her protective older brother. "He likes baseball."

They laughed.

Thinking she'd unwittingly maligned Eddie, she was defensive. "That's why he spends his summers with John in Wisconsin. John's good at ball and works with Eddie on his game. He's coaching a Legion team and Eddie's on it this year even though he's just ten. They're glad to have him on their team. John's gonna come and get him in a car and everything."

She paused, then added convincingly, "But I prefer the Greyhound."

Junior, his eyes like spots of black coal pressed into his round rosy face, glanced quizzically toward Theta. Why, he wondered, did she always insist she liked the worst things? She seemed too smart for that kind of malarkey.

"Say, Theta," he said, trying not to smile, "do you pronounce the capital of Kentucky Loa'vul or Louis-ville?"

"Frankfort," answered Theta, ruining Junior's joke.

Chapter Five

1932

His Story

If he hadn't been carrying the freshly baked blackberry pie, Smiles would have vaulted over his grandmother Mildred's wrought iron fence. Instead, he entered through the gate and carefully secured the latch behind him so Skipper wouldn't bolt into the street.

"Mom!" he shouted as he let himself into his grandmother's front room, followed by the prancing terrier. "Mama sent pie for you and Pop."

Mildred appeared in the kitchen doorway, drying her hands on a dish towel. "Bring it on in and we'll have us a piece."

Smiles laughed, knowing it meant half the pie for him, half for her. "What about Pop?"

"Don't you worry about Grandpa. After we've had our pie and coffee, you can run to the Spudnut and git him some bear claws. You know how Grandpa likes them nuts in the caramel icing. Now cut us each a slice," she said, setting two dinner plates on her kitchen worktable.

Smiles used a butcher knife to divide the pie in two, careful to not let the braided crust crumble onto the sugar-sparkling top crust of the pie. As he lifted half the pie to a Blue Willow dinner plate, he asked, "Mom, you got anything you want me to do?"

"Doesn't your mother have need of you today?" Mildred asked, setting a cup of milky coffee in front of him and taking a seat across the table with her own richly dark Maxwell House.

"No, she's helping Sis and Presh cut out patterns for their school dresses. She said I was lucky to wear overalls and not have to sew new clothes ever' fall."

31

"Oh, I do love to sew," Mildred said. "When your mama was a baby, Grandpa wanted to go move out West . . ."

"Where cowboys are?" Smiles asked, eyes gleaming. He'd heard this story many times before, but loved hearing it again and again, so he asked his grandmother questions as if it were his first time hearing of the hard journey to Kansas.

"No, there wasn't nobody but men a-wantin' to be farmers like your Grandpa did."

"But Pop's not a farmer."

"That's right, he isn't!" she laughed. "But aren't I glad? There was nothing out there but flat land with miles and miles of prairie grass as high as your head, as far as you could see. I just hated it out there."

"You did?" Smiles asked in wonderment around a mouthful of tart pie.

"Oh, I was so homesick for my mama. I wanted to come home so bad. That's what I was a-going to tell you about. I loved to sew and your mama was just two years old. I loved making dresses for her. But we didn't have no room in the wagon . . ."

"A *covered* wagon?" Smiles enthused.

Mildred nodded, not sharing Smiles' excitement. "There wasn't no room for my Singer. But Mama sent it to me after I wrote her a letter saying how much I wished I could make Jacky some new clothes. Along with it she sent material, thread, and embroidering yarn, too. The first thing I made was a little pinafore with ruffled cap sleeves. Made my own pattern out of newspapers Mama sent out. And I smocked the front. Oh, she looked so sweet in that little dress."

Smiles couldn't picture his mother as a toddler. It was as hard to imagine as envisioning his grandparents crossing the plains in a covered wagon. So he asked, "How long'd you stay out there, Mom?"

"Thank goodness not much more than a year. I hated it," she said again. "That very first crop was a disaster. We pert near lost ever'thing 'cause your Grandpa knew as much about farming as he does about making this here pie."

"I'm glad you came back, Mom. I'd a missed you."

Mildred reached out and tweaked his nose.

The plate and pie tin were scraped clean of all but a few crumbles of crust. Smiles and his grandmother lingered over another cup of coffee like chatting neighbors. Finally Smiles asked again, "Ya got any work ya want me to do, Mom?"

"I do!" she said, rising and taking his empty cup.

Smiles rubbed his hands briskly on the thighs of his overalls, ready to get started no matter the task. He gathered the dishes and forks from the table, carried them to the counter near the sink, and met Mildred as she turned from where she'd set the cups.

She reached into her apron pocket and pulled out a quarter. "Now run down to the Spudnut and git yer Grandpa two bear claws. Make sure they was made fresh this morning. I don't have to tell you to bring me back the change. But, Smiles, I want you to keep ten cents for yourself."

"Ten cents!"

"You spend it any way you want."

"Can I get some rolls for me and the fellas?"

"Sweet rolls or anything you want for anybody you want." She laughed.

Smiles found his friends in a vacant lot behind the Spudnut Donut Shop off Ridge Street not far from Sevastopol Elementary School. Though tall grass camouflaged the gang's ornery shenanigans, he knew at a glance that they were preparing another practical joke for Louie's little brother Bud. Francis had just finished contributing to the orange soda when Smiles came around the corner of the neighborhood store. Buttoning the barn door of his dungarees, Francis was gingerly holding a half-empty Nehi bottle between his thumb and forefinger.

He elbowed a disheveled boy next to him. "Take it!"

Each boy took his turn contributing urine then handing the filling bottle one to the other. The five ruffians stood in a semicircle, urging each other on until the yellowing orange soda came back to Francis. Giggling with anticipation, he held the glass bottle out to Smiles.

"Aw, I don't know," Smiles said shoving his hands into the pockets of his overalls. "I think you got enough in there already. 'Sides, Mom give me a dime. I'm gonna go get us some rolls."

Ignoring his friends' pleas to first join in their joke, Smiles ran to the front of the crackerbox wood-slatted store. Just as he was about to open the Spudnut's squeaking screen door, he spotted Bud pulling a rattling Flyer toward the bakery. The rusted wagon protested with every sidewalk crack. Smiles waited until the boy looked up, then motioned him over.

"Hey, kid, want a roll? I'm buyin'."

When he and the younger boy emerged from the store, biting into caramel iced crullers, the other boys were milling around on the sidewalk, kicking dust, holding in laughter as they strove to appear innocent. Louie held the contaminated soda.

"Here," Smiles said, offering the sack of rolls to Bud's brother. "I'll give 'im the Nehi."

A knowing smile growing as he saw Smiles had corralled Bud, Louie handed over the bottle. Smiles released his grip on the tainted orange soda as he passed the donut sack to his friend. The bottle fell between them, crashing to the sidewalk. Glass and fizzing liquid sprayed a pale orange starburst. In an eruption of disappointed groans, the boys jumped back as if the spray were battery acid.

"Oh, man, look at that!" Smiles said, frowning at the waste. "And I was just about to offer it to little Bud here, too."

Smiles was a head taller than the other boys, a scholastic year behind most of them. Quarantined with his sisters, who had scarlet fever the previous fall, he'd missed too much school to catch up. The result was that he bridged the gap between boys his own age and younger neighborhood kids. His easy disposition and athletic prowess were intrinsic magnets that attracted both groups. His ability to make each boy feel singularly important held them fast. So no one thought to blame him when the loaded Nehi sprayed its foul liquid over their bare feet.

Instead, they were easily distracted by three budding teenage girls sashaying toward them arm-in-arm. The girls would have lifted their pretty chins in haughty disdain if they hadn't seen Smiles at the center of the bedraggled group. He grinned and prepared to motion them around the tainted sidewalk when he saw Francis turning awkward cartwheels in the uneven brick street, successfully gaining the girls' attention.

"Watch what I can do," Smiles said loudly to his friends as if he hadn't seen the trio, their plaid skirts swaying to their gait.

He glanced from the corners of his eyes without turning his head to be sure the girls were still watching Francis, then approached a splintering utility pole dark with tar. Francis landed hard on his rump as Smiles spit on his hands then jumped onto the massive round pole, circling it with his legs and arms.

Francis dusted his britches, shielded his eyes with a calloused palm, and squinted toward the electric wires twenty feet overhead. Smiles inched up the pole like a monkey after a coconut. The other boys clapped their hands and hooted, urging him upward.

As Smiles reached the top of the pole just as the girls,

pretending disinterest, entered the Spudnut, he reached out to claim his prize.

Chapter Six

1934

His Story

Everyone said it was a miracle he'd only broken his arms. If the volts of electricity didn't kill him, the fall should have. Smiles had landed on his back in the middle of the bricked street, well away from the pole he'd just climbed. Francis had stood immobile, his eyes half dollars of frightened disbelief as he squatted to stare down at the unconscious Smiles.

"Are ya dead? Hey, Smiles, wake up, will ya?!"

Bud tugged at Louie's limp arm. "We gotta git Miz Smythe. C'mon!"

The two bolted as the others gathered around Smiles, who lay motionless at dusty, calloused feet. They marveled at the boy's upturned lips.

"He smiles even when he's dyin'!" Francis said in an awed whisper.

"Yeah," responded a hushed, impressed chorus.

Being spared the ordeal of coming upon a scene that by all reason should have been fatal, Jacky had found her son blinking his eyes, rising to consciousness within a circle of youngsters. He studied his impressed audience, including three weeping girls. His eyes passed over them, searching for something infinitely more desirable.

"Where'd the man go?" he finally wondered aloud.

Before the boys could ask who he meant, they were parted by Jacky pushing through their tight circle. "Gracious, Miles! You can thank the good Lord you're alive. What was you tryin' to prove goin' up that telephone pole? Bud said you touched them hot wires, too!"

She bent to take hold of his elbows to help him up but recoiled as he howled at the touch.

"Sorry, mama. I guess I must've hurt my arms. Say, why's Grandpa's rolls laying there in the street? Did ya drop 'em or something, Bud? Well, I guess that's all right. We can get him more."

Smiles had spent the rest of the summer with both arms in casts, which caused injury to his dignity far beyond the growing tale of his ill-fated attempt to grab attention rather than live electrical wires. By the time he entered Dennis Junior High School two years later, the episode had become a legend and a joke.

"Showin' off for some girls." Francis laughed, emphasizing the last as he again recounted the incident to the gang walking toward the brick school two neighborhoods from Sevastopol. "Couldn't wipe his own ass for two months!"

More laughter as others joined in. The boys never tired of bringing up their story. For they believed it belonged to them; they'd witnessed Smiles reaching for glory but instead catapulting backward before hurtling twenty feet to hit the bricks full on his back. And only two broken bones to show for all of that. It was a wonder.

At the moment, Smiles wasn't smarting from the teasing that came with the others' boasts. He was wincing from the leather vise of stiff new shoes. The first few days of the fall term he'd successfully hidden the new Buster Browns under the stoop at Quigley's Market, but he didn't dare do it again.

He suspected Presh had seen and tattled, but he couldn't blame her. It was, after all, his lie. During last night's strapping, he'd tried to convince his belt-wielding father that only sissies didn't go barefoot to school. Porter, his breath reeking of Nola Kent's bootleg, and swinging the belt with ever more force, convinced him otherwise.

"Ah, dang," Louie muttered, cutting his laughter short as he lowered his head and dug balled hands into his overall pockets.

They were coming up the hill to the junior high school where a throng of students clustered near arched doorways waiting for the morning bell. But walking toward them, swaggering with the menace of upperclassmen, was a group whose intentions were clear. It was the custom of ninth grade boys to haze seventh graders, not to be confused with a somewhat more friendly initiation of a fraternity.

They'd been gunning for the popular Fairview boy, the one who was nearly their own size, and here he was delivering himself like Isaac to the stone sacrifice.

"Hey, Smithie," called one, thinking himself clever to mispronounce Smiles' Anglican family name.

The others in this older group laughed at the mean joke. They weren't so different from Smiles' friends; they all came from working class families struggling to survive the Depression. But these boys lived on the other side of Main Street closer to Earlham College, so felt the privilege of having a slight advantage.

They'd already initiated most other boys coming into the seventh grade, all except for Eddie Whittle who'd received unrequested amnesty due to his ballfield prowess. And now they were ready for bigger game.

Smiles' demeanor belied the tightening of his stomach as dread manipulated that automatic reflex. Shifting his books to rest easily on his hip, he lightly slipped his right hand into his pocket. He appeared to stroll unafraid toward them, his back straight and his knees effortlessly bending into a sauntering gait.

A half block from the promised confrontation, he nodded his chin in friendly recognition and widened his smile. He suppressed the hard swallow knotting his throat and was about to call "Hello, fellas" when the school's call to order rang from the belfry.

"Saved by the bell," Louie breathed, his eyes still on his ragged toenails.

All day Smiles knew that the bell would sound again, this time signaling an end to his uneasy reprieve. Each time he passed one of the menacing freshmen in the hall between classes, he was careful to maintain nonchalance however harsh the upperclassman's lowered shoulder caused him to momentarily lose balance. Scurrying to keep up, his friends ducked as if avoiding a shadow blow, then looked to him for reassurance that never failed.

At lunchtime, Smiles bravely faced his tormentors who gestured harm with eyes and clenched fists from their exclusive table across the gymnasium. He struggled to imperceptibly swallow his bologna sandwich and gulp lukewarm milk from a pint bottle his mother had packed hours earlier. No one would have guessed his anxiety.

If English literature followed by grammar weren't agony enough, Smiles' dread progressed along with the Seth Thomas' minute hand marching toward his hour of reckoning. His eyes trained on the maddeningly martial movement of the clock rather than Miss Dillon's scratching on the blackboard. It seemed both an eternity and an instant before the final bell sounded.

Pushing through the school's double doors, Smiles could see the older boys waiting for him a half block away, leaning against a stone wall that held in place someone's terraced lawn. Flanked by Louie and Francis, who imperceptibly slipped behind him, Smiles maintained eye contact and walked determinedly toward his doom. The vigilant upperclassmen shifted away from their ragged stone support and meandered importantly toward the Fairview boys.

"You're all right," one of them said to Smiles, smirking.

"Yeah," said another. "Some fellas from shop class told us you're on their Legion team. They say you're all right. And you hit homers clean over Clear Creek.

"How are ya at basketball?"

Chapter Seven

1935

Her Story

Eddie Whittle had forgone the rare extravagance of a Saturday matinee. He and Smiles Smythe had been the only seventh graders recruited to join Dennis' ninth grade basketball team, so he'd gone to practice in the school's overheated gymnasium instead of joining his sisters and mother at the Tivoli movie theater.

Theta wished he'd come with them to the movies. She didn't realize that his absence had secured the indulgence. Their mother had managed to save four dimes but not five. Though there wasn't change for popcorn or a bus to and from the downtown theater, seeing *The Gold Diggers of 1933* was treat enough. That was, until they stepped from the warmth of the Tivoli Theater into the bite of February's bitter tempest.

Camille and Marlene skipped ahead as Theta trudged beside her mother through the fresh snow that'd begun to cover the sidewalks while she was laughing in the dark at Ginger Rogers singing pig Latin. It crunched under their feet, testament to the dipping temperatures stinging her nostrils. Butting her head into the wind, she tightened her hold on her mother's hand, urging May Nelle to hurry.

Again she wished Eddie had come along. He would have held her other hand, keeping it warm. No matter how she hunched inside Marlene's discarded tweed coat or curled her fingers in the torn lining of its pocket, her left hand was stiff with cold. The fingers entwined in her mother's had long since lost feeling.

Camille and Marlene inserted stomps into their skips to keep the blood flowing in their toes. Hardly anyone they knew had fur-lined overshoes these Depression years, but at least most girls and boys had rubbers to keep the snow from invading thin leather. Theta tried wiggling her toes but succeeded only in stumbling as she clumsily dug loose soles into frozen ground.

Though her tingling ears were tucked tightly beneath a wool scarf, Theta heard a car's horn and raised her head to see her brother Mark's secondhand Oldsmobile coming toward them across the Doran Bridge. Relieved, she waved as if flagging down a rescue plane. Her sister-in-law Georgeanne leaned across Mark and giddily flapped her hand as they sped past, the car horn a receding staccato.

Theta's arm and hopeful smile dropped. The girls and their mother were still more than a freezing mile from home. The image of Mark pumping his hand against the steering wheel to blare a perceived taunt as Georgeanne with her Cheshire grin waved dismissal, was instantly seared into her mind and memory.

Theta looked to her mother for explanation but May Nelle's lips were tucked tightly together so that only the generous flesh of her angry chin was visible to the little girl. Though she couldn't see them, Theta knew her mother's eyes were narrowed in indignation bordering on wrath. She quickly looked away, afraid that she would be blamed for Mark driving by without mercifully stopping to give a lift to his lumbering mother or his littlest sisters. Unconsciously, she mimicked her mother's jutted jaw and squinted with fractious eyebrows in resentful ire. She hated him; and the gloating Georgeanne even more.

"It's not us, Mom," she said into the unforgiving wind. "It's them. They're just jealous we've been to the movies without them."

The kitchen was toasty compared to outside. May Nelle ran

cool water over her daughters' hands as the girls crowded together to hold them over the chipped enamel sink. Tears streaked their chapped cheeks as needles and pins returned to numb fingers. Theta was sucking the tips of both hands, her saliva renewing life, when the back door banged open against the pie safe.

"Aun' Nola!" the girls cried as their mother's cousin rushed in with a delighted squeal.

Nola laughed as she dusted snow from her beaver coat. "It's a white Christmas!"

Theta heard Nola drop the last syllable along with her smile and felt ashamed. Around her fingers she said as convincingly as possible, "We're glad, too."

"Good Lord," Nola said, taking Theta's fingers from her mouth and briskly rubbing them in a circular motion between her own soft palms. "This child's hands are raw as hamburger. Didja forget your gloves, honey?"

"We don't have any," Camille offered, showing her own hands to the woman they considered an aunt, since she'd at one time been married to May Nelle's brother, Gilbert. The two older Whittle girls were unaware that the marriage had been outside acceptable norms of society. In their innocence Nola was a brilliant light in their otherwise gloomy existence. Only Theta, who was so quiet that her mother dismissed any idea that she heard or understood her angry gossip, knew the circumstances of the cousins' marriage.

"Here, look at Marlene's," Camille said. "They're all red, too."

Nola dropped Theta's hands to inspect the other girls'. Theta assessed her own, noting that, with the coat of cruel chafing, they were actually more of a dusty pink. With a disappointed scowl directed at Marlene, she stood back, awed by the woman bent over her sister.

Though she was scandalous: divorced—divorced!—and rich from bootlegging, Nola was Theta's ideal. Independent, smart, wealthy. She had her own apartment, was always dressed as if she'd stepped from a band box, and oh, she smelled so wonderful. Sweet and luxurious.

Nola was pulling a milky glass bottle from her oversized leather purse. She unscrewed the cap and turned it over Marlene's hand. Rich white lotion poured from the bottle into the child's palm. Nola instructed the girl to rub her hands together as if washing. She moved on to Camille.

When it was Theta's turn, Nola dabbed the lotion onto the backs of her small, still-icy hands then gently rubbed the thick, creamy lotion into the rough, chapped skin herself. The lotion aggravated the stinging in her hands, but Theta didn't mind. Aunt Nola's fingertips felt as smooth as the kid gloves she'd earlier removed.

Theta had never experienced anything so lovingly tender.

"My goodness, honey, your cheeks are just as raw as your mitts. Let's rub a little of this lotion on them, too, shall we? Here, sugar, look up."

Theta lifted her face, closed her eyes, and breathed deeply the aroma she always associated with her Aunt Nola. Though her chafed skin burned as lotion penetrated minute cracks in her raw cheeks, she could barely suppress a self-conscious smile. She took careful note of the bottle's black and white label: Jergen's Lotion.

"Now, May Nelle," Nola said in her smooth Louisville drawl, "I need to take this sugar pie home to help me eat up some ham 'n beans I got left over from last Sat'day. You just know they'll go bad if I don't. I'll carry her on back in the mornin'."

Camille and Marlene brightened. Their mother, they knew

for certain, would never allow it. Theta had never spent an evening, let alone a whole night, out of their mother's demanding sight. But they could.

"I don't mind helping Aun' Nola, Mom," Camille hurriedly offered, a slight sacrifice.

Marlene slipped her arm around her older sister's waist. "Me, too!"

Nola patted their heads. "Why, May Nelle, don't you have just the sweetest girls in the worl'? Both so willin' to come over home to help out. And me with a dozen dress shirts to iron." She pronounced the last word "arn."

Assuming a serious tone, she continued, "They'll be just the help I need. You know how bad I am at that sort of thing. Why, what a relief it is to know I'll have these two sugar dumplin's to arn all those dress shirts."

Theta retreated to the scarred child's chair May Nelle kept for her in the kitchen. She was lightly rubbing her left hand with gentle fingers just as Nola had done, focused on the task as if she couldn't hear her sisters maneuvering to take her proffered place. Like them, she knew her mother would never allow her to go, so she didn't hate them too much for it.

Concentrating on rubbing her hands together, she muttered with conviction, "Ham and beans. I'd rather have the apple jelly I helped Mom put up last summer anyway. And I'll slice the bread real thick. Camille and Marlene can have dumb ham 'n beans. I'd rather stay here and eat my own supper. And just let them iron those shirts. They won't do near the good job *I'd* do."

She was so engrossed by her silent argument, Theta didn't hear Camille and Marlene change their minds.

"Now I think about it," Camille said, speaking for both of them, "the walk home made me awful tired." She pronounced the last word "tarred" just as Nola would.

"Maybe," Marlene chimed in, "we should stay to home; as much as we'd just love to come help press them shirts, of course. Ain't that right, Camille?"

Theta did, however, hear Aunt Nola express mock disappointment.

While her sisters missed the sarcasm, she recognized the playful lilt in Nola's appeal. "May Nelle, what am I to do? I just have to have at least one of these girls come give me a han'."

Theta couldn't help but allow her tightly pressed lips to twitch in amusement when she saw her sisters' faces drop as her mother said sternly, "Camille, Marlene, you go git your nightclothes."

Nola said quickly, "May Nelle Kent Cook Whittle, I have never known you to be selfish. You just heard me say I've got a dozen dress shirts to arn and you're not going to let me take Theta, who's been ironing right alongside you for years? Nobody presses dress shirts like you. Why, this child has learned from the master. Now, are you going to let me take Theta for the night or not? I'll carry her back home right after dinner tomorrow. Cross my heart. She'll have plenty of time to finish them shirts by then.

"And of course I'll pay whatever your customers give."

That did it, as both Theta and Aunt Nola knew it would. May Nelle huffed at the insult. "You will *not* pay to have them shirts ironed! Theta, go git your nightclothes."

Nola picked up her kid gloves from the cracked linoleum countertop where she'd tossed them. Camille and Marlene rushed from the kitchen before their mother could reconsider. Theta followed them, hurrying to get her nightdress for the same reason.

In the front seat of Aunt Nola's Ford Coupe, Theta held her

hands tightly in her lap. Not because they were cold, but because she was afraid they might flutter and dance like the frenzied butterflies in her stomach. She also held her grin tightly in check, fearing if she allowed it to burst through her lips she'd never stop laughing.

This was her first excursion. She had never slept away from her mother. Had never, in fact, spent more than a few moments outside school or church further than a few feet from her. And now to be sleeping in Aunt Nola's apartment! Theta felt that her heart would burst with outright adoration for this woman in the soft leather gloves humming along with the car radio.

"Aun' Nola," she said when the tune ended, "I'm real good at ironing shirts. The secret's in where you start."

"Is that right?"

"Yes," Theta said knowingly. "Most people do one front first then the back and then the other front and then the arms and collar. But the trick is to do the collar and arms first, then the two front panels, and the back last so's you don't get it wrinkled moving around the rest on the ironing board."

Nola laughed, having seen for the very first time the girl's overlapped front teeth as Theta smiled through her serious discourse. She almost sounded like an old maid schoolteacher giving a lecture, Nola thought with amusement.

There had been no shyness about Theta's ironing instructions. Nola hoped there would be no bashfulness when they stopped by the Hoosier Store for Theta to choose pairs of mittens for herself and her sisters. Nola patted Theta's hand reassuringly.

"Oh, Theta, you're such an old little girl." But even as she marveled at the girl's rare grin, Nola saw it disappear.

"I'm not old, Aun' Nola," she said as if her aunt should be

aware that fourth graders were light years from the privileged rank of sixth graders at her elementary school. "I'm nine."

"Going on twenty-nine! But I'm not laughing at you, sweetheart. Except, don't you know that your mother, your two big sisters, and you, too, my bright little bulb, seem to have forgotten something?"

Nola could hardly continue through her chortles. "Y'all know I don't have a husban' or a man I'm beholdin' to. So, why on earth would I have dress shirts to arn?"

Theta's heart leapt as she realized with genuine wonder that someone – this magnificent woman with her head thrown back, hooting with unrestrained glee –actually loved her.

Chapter Eight

1937-38

Her Story

Uncle Honey and Aunt Shirlee had taken Theta along with their growing brood to the Jefferson County fair on the outskirts of Louisville. Both had dismissed with waves of hands and laughter May Nelle's demand that her daughter keep her company back at the cabin. They laughed even harder when May Nelle, who earlier proclaimed she wouldn't go for the life of her anywhere near all that dust and manure, argued with conviction, "I'm not going to the fair, so why should she?"

Shirlee, her laughter subsiding as she realized May Nelle's faulty rationale was quite serious, had said that she could hardly allow her own children to go to the fair when another was left behind.

"That just wouldn't be right." She pronounced the last word "rat" but in a way that seemed to leave the decision up to May Nelle: either all the children would go, or none.

Theta was at last given permission to accompany her cousins and their parents. But in a final move to assert her authority, May Nelle had insisted that Theta not ride in the open-air back of the 1924 Model T pick-up truck with the older children, but instead squeeze into the cab with Uncle Honey, Aunt Shirlee, and the two youngest Kent children.

The argument with May Nelle had caused them to be only a little late to a special presentation in the fairground's band shell of Fannie R. Buchanan's latest musical performed by the local 4-H orchestra. Theta, who considered herself more intelligent and knowledgeable than her hill cousins, squirmed uncomfortably on the cement riser, but not because her seat was hard as a rock. Her ego was feeling a might pained.

While she had never heard of the National Boys and Girls Club News that published Buchanan's songs and sponsored 4-H music appreciation efforts across the nation, her Kentucky kin, right down to little Josephine, were fans of the newspaper and its programs.

"Ever' first Sat'day we listen to music like this on WAVE radio. It comes outta Hopkinsville and lasts a whole hour!" Junior informed Theta, pronouncing the last word "ar."

Mistakenly thinking to further impress his northern cousin, he added, "It's edge-cational."

After the performance, Theta followed the chattering Kent family as they slowly made their way with other enthusiastic fans from the amphitheater. Outside they paused as Uncle Honey gave each child, including Theta, a precious dime to spend on the midway.

He shook a gnarled index finger as if in reprimand. "Now you kids stay together. Junior, Theta, y'all are almost teenagers, so you keep an eye on these little 'uns. We'll meet up at the south end of the midway in two ars. Don't ya'll leave the lights of the midway, hear?"

Holding hands in groups of two and three, the children skipped toward the twinkling yellow bulbs strung across a wide dirt path beaten into the disappearing grass. On either side of this created midway were small canvas tents. Some were three-sided with brightly lit interiors featuring games of skill or chance. Others were mysterious, their flaps closed to the curious, promising scandalous attractions such as belly dancers and human oddities. At the end of the midway, thrilling rides bejeweled with twinkling multi-colored bulbs beckoned.

Though reluctant to part with the first money she'd ever held, Theta was drawn to a water-stained tent near the entrance to the midway. It sat back, vaguely hidden in the dark. Its canvas door was partially, invitingly open. She abruptly stopped, causing younger cousins behind to bump into her and one another. A weathered sign featuring a crystal ball proclaiming in fancy letters "Fortunes!" leaned against the discolored tent. For a nickel, a bona fide gypsy would tell your future.

"You'll use half yer money on just one thing," Junior reasoned, pulling Theta's hand. "And not the best at that. Let's git us some cotton caindy and ride the Ferris wheel. You can see a hundred miles from the top!"

"I just got to know, Junior, what my future holds. It'll give me hope to know I'll have a job where I dress up and live in my very own apartment. And that I'm going to college and travel on vacations! It would just make all the difference to know I've got that to look forward to. And if I don't have all that in store for me, well, if I don't, I've just got to know so I can be brave to make the best of it.

"But, Junior," she said, her eyes bright, "what if I do? What if the fortuneteller tells me I'll have all that in store? Then I'll be able to, well, I can . . ."

"For somebody so smart, you sure are dumb sometimes, Theta. That lady ain't real. She's just gonna pretend to see somethin' in that glass ball o' hers. And 'sides, we done learned in Sunday School we shouldn't have no truck with things like this. It leads to no-good 'cause if it is real, that lady gets her pa'r from the devil."

He shivered his fear and distaste as he attempted to pull Theta toward the brighter lights illuminating the midway. "Come ride the rides with me. They're just two cents."

Theta shook her head. "You go on. I'll catch up."

Junior gave her a disgusted look and crossed his arms. "Naw. I'll go with ya. Daddy'd give me what-for if I was to leave you alone with them gypsies. Turn-about's fair play anyhow 'cause now you'll have to wait for me to finish goin' on all them rides. You won't have but a nickel left and y'all won't have hardly enough for cotton caindy neither."

He hoped with these last statements that Theta would see reason and go along with him and his siblings. But her mind was made up the moment she saw the tantalizing sign with the message that promised both foretelling and favor: Fortunes.

As Theta began to duck inside, Junior reluctantly turned to his brothers and sisters with the admonition, "Y'all stay here. Don't move a inch and keep aholt of each other. We'll be out shortly."

The gypsy looked real enough, with wiry gray hair escaping a colorful paisley bandana. Golden hoops pulled at her drooping earlobes and a mass of shining beads lay in tangled ropes over beleaguered breasts. With Junior standing just over her shoulder, Theta sat in a wobbly wooden folding chair. She placed the dime on what appeared to be a folding table draped with a fringed shawl.

The old woman placed a palm over the silver and moved it tight against the tabletop to the edge then pushed a tarnished nickel toward Theta. Without pronouncement or delay, she took Theta's right hand in both her own. Breathing deeply and exhaling with a rasp, the gypsy examined the girl's palm as if she couldn't quite make out the map creased in a spider web across the tender flesh.

Finally she said with considerable authority, "Hmm. I see that before the year isss out you will meet the boy that isss to be your hussband."

Theta jerked her hand from the fortune teller's grasp as if stung by a serpent. She hadn't considered that she might someday go from one shared bed to another. To yet another kitchen and a different form of servitude. She was crestfallen. It couldn't be that college and career would be denied for husband and housekeeping.

"Are you sure?"

"The lines don't lie, leetle geerl. It's right here," the gypsy said, jabbing a sharp fingernail into Theta's palm and tapping pointedly. "If you wish to know more, you weell have to give me another five cents."

Theta nodded and returned the nickel despite Junior's harrumphed disapproval. "How will I know it's him when I meet him?"

The gypsy brought a cloudy glass globe the size of a grapefruit to the center of the card table and looked dully into it, caressing its invisible aura. "I weel tell you only theesss on the nickel: I see pillars holding up a low ceiling in a very large room with small high windows. There are long curtains. The boy that weel be your . . ."

She seemed perplexed then continued, "The curtains. They are not for the windows so high up. And I see glass baskets hanging from the ceiling. This is where you meet heem."

Her eyes widened. Moving the globe swiftly aside, she took from her pocket a dime and tossed it across the table.

Alarmed, Theta grabbed Junior's wrist as she stared wide-eyed from the displaced globe to the woman. "What did you see?"

"I no want you money," the gypsy said, shaking her head and waving both hands. "It's ordained."

"Ordained?"

The old woman made the sign of a cross and kissed the tips of her wrinkled fingers. "There is also crosss. I no take you money, leetle geerl."

"But how will I know it's him?"

The gypsy impatiently motioned with both hands, shooing the two preteens from her tent.

Junior grabbed the dime from the table and pulled Theta to her feet. "Let's get out of here!"

Later that night, lying on the tattered quilt behind the barn staring at constellations with her cousins, Theta wondered, "Where do you think this place is, Junior? The place with the curtains that aren't for windows? Where in the world do glass baskets hang from a low ceiling?"

"And 'crosss'," he laughed. "Don't forget the crosss."

"Don't make fun of me. You sure did make a beeline out of there. What were you so scared of if you didn't believe what she said?"

"That old woman was crazy or downright evil, that's what. You're lucky she didn't do somethin' awful to ya. Might've, too, if I hadn't a-been there."

"I believe her, Junior. I saw her eyes. She was spooked."

"I seen her, too, and I don't think she was puttin' on a show. No matter how funny she talked or how crazy. We didn't have no bizness goin' in there."

"How come she gave back my money?"

Junior was quiet a moment before he allowed, "I don't know why she give it back. Maybe she was using you to drum up more bizness. She prob'ly does this ever' night; have her first customer go out and tell people what she done. Y'all was her shill."

"Her shell?"

"You know; the local rube who brings in more bizness."

Theta pondered this, then said with confidence, "Maybe. But I believe she was really seeing something. And you know what I think? I think she was seeing a church in that crystal ball 'cause of the cross. And it's gotta be a basement room on account of the high up windows and low ceiling. The only thing is, I don't understand what those curtains and baskets are."

When she returned to her Hoosier home from Kentucky, Theta began to scout churches of every denomination in and around her Baxter neighborhood. After broadening her search, just as she'd begun to lose hope after nearly a year of searching, she stumbled onto Trinity Methodist Church in Fairview.

It was a stucco building painted a curious pink. She kneeled to peek into a basement window and saw that its shadowy room was strung with wires from one wall to the other. Heavy cotton curtains hung from them, pulled back to open the space. A table that looked like it'd once been in someone's dining room stood against the far wall. On it was a small wooden cross.

"This has to be it," she murmured as she braced herself against the rough cement of the church to stand.

The next Sunday Theta prepared a special breakfast of gravy and Clabber Girl biscuits for Eddie. He came into the kitchen already dressed to attend the Lutheran church down the block. Its baseball team was one of the best in the city-wide Church League and Eddie never missed a Sunday if he wanted to take the field with the starting line-up the following Saturday.

"Boy oh boy," he said, delighted, when Theta set the biscuits and gravy on the table. "It's not my birthday is it?"

Theta shook her head. "You know it's not, Eddie. But I made this special for you 'cause I was hoping you'd take me to church today."

"You don't have to bribe me to do that."

"To Trinity over in Fairview."

"Nope. Can't do it. We got a game next weekend. If I'm not in church today, I won't be playing first innings. Maybe none of 'em unless they're fallin' way behind."

Eddie opened two biscuits onto his plate and ladled a healthy helping of gravy onto them. "Whatcha wanna go over there for anyway? The Lutherans have a good Sunday school class."

Theta knew that as soon as she heard fork against china, May Nelle would make her appearance. Anxiously she bit her lip then made a quick decision. "Eddie, I've gotta go to that church and it has to be now. I don't think I should put it off. It's got to be that church and it's gotta be today."

"Today? What for?" Eddie sounded slightly alarmed.

Embarrassed, Theta was grieved to tell about the fortune teller's prediction but knew that Eddie could be as stubborn as their mother. "Last summer I went to the fair with Junior and we went in a gypsy's tent. Just for fun, of course. But she told me I was going to find something in a church basement that would change my life. She described Trinity to a T, so it's gotta be there and nowhere else. I'm sure of it. She said I'd find it before the year was out, and the year's almost up!"

She took a breath and leaned expectantly toward her brother, glancing anxiously at the doorway. May Nelle would surely step through it any minute.

Eddie scraped the plate with his fork, licking the last of the gravy from its tines. "You believe that nonsense, do ya, Tooey?"

Theta nodded, her eyes pleading.

"Okay. Just this once, though."

Later, when Camille and Marlene realized that Eddie would be devoting an entire morning to the special outing with Theta, they too decided to give the Methodist church a try. Besides, it was an excellent opportunity to also spend a rare hour with their usually aloof brother. Eddie would normally ditch the girls before entering their neighborhood church, but he'd not leave them alone in an unfamiliar building.

Arriving at the Fairview church, Camille and Marlene quickly fell in with a group of girls they knew from school and soon discovered two of them were the younger sisters of Smiles Smythe. It occurred to them both at once—Trinity's youth group would be a perfect social outlet, one without dues or fees.

Theta picked up a Sunday school book and found a folding chair near the table with the cross. She sat uneasily on the flimsy chair, her back straight. She pretended to read while glancing over the top of the paper booklet to measure the probability that her future husband might be among the gaggle of ruffians tossing around wadded hymnal pages. She hoped not.

Eddie lounged behind and to the left of Theta, appearing to be serious though smiling within. He'd never known Theta to be anything if not pragmatic. He didn't believe in that gypsy mumbo-jumbo but wouldn't deny his quiet sister's unusual folly. She was rarely so insistent. Or gullible. If this morning's request hadn't been so atypical, he wouldn't have agreed to forego his place on the starting line-up this Saturday.

He was musing over what it might be that she was so sure would be here for her when he saw Smiles crossing the room toward them. Theta saw him, too, and quickly lowered her eyes.

Waiting for worship service to end in the sanctuary above, Smiles had been listening for the organ doxology when he noticed Eddie across the crowded basement. Convicted as if he'd fallen to the road to Damascus instead of to the bricks in front of the neighborhood bakery, Smiles rarely missed a Sunday at the little neighborhood church. His friends naturally followed him to Sunday school, and then his sisters, as they approached adolescence, just as naturally followed his friends. The church's youth attendance had ballooned, and its basketball and baseball teams flourished.

As Smiles walked toward Eddie, he could barely keep from

staring at the younger girl holding a faded lesson book like a renaissance mask. Only her eyes showed above it. And then she lowered the booklet.

Her resemblance to Eddie was unmistakable. A familiar yet alien pang shot through Smile's chest. No wonder Eddie hovered protectively; the poor girl was obviously uncomfortably shy. Pushing Francis away with a laugh as his friend attempted to catch a wadded paper ball made from a torn page, Smiles walked toward the brother and sister. Eddie shifted from the cement block wall and met Smiles' hand with a firm grasp.

Theta, her eyes steadfastly studying the text before her, overheard the boys talking about Trinity's baseball team. Smiles was inviting her brother to join. Images of watching their games flashed through her mind and she pressed her lips against the pleasure of the thought, before hearing Eddie beg off.

"I'll soon be going to Wisconsin to join my brother's Legion team, so I may as well stay on with the Lutherans."

Catching her bottom lip with her overlapping front teeth, Theta continued to scan the Sunday school book, but instead of black serif words on yellowing newsprint, she saw Kentucky bluegrass. When John came for Eddie, she would accompany her mother to their hill cousins' after first dropping Camille and Marlene in Louisville. Trinity would be far in the distance.

Theta lifted her eyes almost imperceptibly and watched Smiles rejoin his friends. As he walked away, she could see the outline of his undershirt beneath his thin cotton dress shirt. She sighed, knowing that as improbable as the gypsy's talent to foretell the future, the probability that her prediction was popular Smiles Smythe was as likely as a Polish Pope. Besides, she saw no baskets anywhere in the room.

"It's just as well," she sighed. "The last thing I want is a husband. I want to be on my own, have a career and my own car. And an apartment."

"Huh?" Eddie asked, his brows knit.

As they hiked from Fairview to Baxter following Sunday school, Eddie flung an arm over Theta's shoulder. "Did you find what you were looking for, Tooey?"

She shook her head, frowning.

"So what's the plan now? You going to drag me to every church in Richmond?"

Camille, walking ahead, stopped to face them. "We're staying at Trinity."

Marlene nodded agreement. "What'd you mean about Theta dragging you to every church in Richmond? What's that all about?"

"Nothing," Eddie said.

Though Trinity's basement fit the gypsy's description, all except for those mysterious baskets, Theta had to admit that Junior was right; she couldn't imagine just who among this morning's rag tag group of adolescents could possibly cause her to forfeit her fervent dream of independence.

Nevertheless, she said as if resigned, "If Camille and Marlene want to keep going to Trinity, I guess I will, too."

With their sisters again walking ahead, Eddie whispered to Theta, "You aren't making any sense. This morning you were bound and determined to find this place. You say Trinity's not it, but now all of a sudden you don't care?"

A little louder and much more gruffly, Eddie said, "I wish I'd known that before I gave up first-string."

"I'm sorry," Theta said quietly, feeling the sting of her brother's rare admonishment but careful to not expose the strange elation that signaled her first crush.

Chapter Nine

1938

His and Her Story

Fidgeting seventh graders filled the first nine rows of Dennis Junior High School's auditorium. Typical of their age group, they resembled little children compared to the upperclassmen toward the back where Eddie sat a safe distance from Camille though they were in the same homeroom. Sandwiched between were eighth graders, where Marlene sat smoothing the dress Camille had outgrown.

Theta, watching her sisters prepare for the first day of school that September morning, was thankful the pair was so persnickety about their appearance. The dress would look almost new when it was her turn and, she thought as she pulled on a thrice-darned anklet, broken in. *Just the way I prefer.*

Even without the physical contrasts between the upper and lowerclassmen, Theta still appeared small as she sat hunched in the oak flip chair, striving to be invisible. As her homeroom filed into the auditorium, she'd noticed the slatted folding chairs on the stage, arranged in a half moon behind a sturdy oak lectern, but now she stared at her hands folded tightly in her lap. She didn't see the students and teachers coming from offstage to fill those seats.

Theta kept her head and eyes lowered until she heard a cacophony of pounding flip-seats as three-hundred students stood *en masse* to face the American flag. Following the Pledge of Allegiance, after the students in the echoing auditorium had resumed their seats with resounding clatter, Mr. Rivir introduced the school's new student body president, Miles Smythe.

Theta quickly glanced up, her face reddening as she followed from under lowered lids Smiles rising from his chair.

Wearing the same light cotton shirt as he did in church, but with a tie choking his thick neck, Smiles approached the lectern with a confidence that belied his nervousness at the prospect of addressing Dennis' massive student body. He grinned out over his audience as he clenched the slanted sides of the dais with his Golden Gloves grip.

"Thank you," he began in an even tone as if he were speaking directly to each student, "for electing me . . ."

He faltered as he caught sight of Eddie's little sister in the first row. Her eyes were locked on his. His grin widened. After a moment of alarm, Theta quickly looked away. Smiles lost his train of thought as he noticed how unhappy she looked. He remembered how frightened he'd been as a seventh grader.

From the back, somewhere in the ninth-grade section, a cracking voice hollered, "What? Electing you what?"

Smiles didn't ignore his contemporaries' gales but joined them, his even teeth gleaming like ivory as he laughed.

Her face burning, Theta turned to stare menacingly over her shoulder toward the hundreds of gleefully chortling faces behind her.

Sue Paul, sitting beside Theta, elbowed her. "I think Smiles Smythe just looked at you!"

Now that she was in junior high school and out of the Baxter neighborhood where her mother could so easily keep her constrained, Theta had determined to make a friend. She'd heard Camille and Marlene talk about this girlfriend and that, though she'd never met any of them. If they could have friends, she was determined that she could, too. Better ones.

She knew the minute she saw Sue in the Dennis Junior High

School library that she fit the bill. If the girl's glasses weren't evidence of superior intellect, the armful of books was. Theta was surprised by how easy it had been to strike up the friendship, unaware that as soon as she introduced herself as a Whittle the deal was sealed. Somehow, by what miracle she didn't know, she found Sue sitting next to her at every turn.

Theta turned so quickly to her new friend that she still glowered. Recovering, she hid a pleased smile with her hand. "If he did, it was just an accident. We go to the same church. He probably recognized me. He came over to talk to Eddie the first time we went there."

Sue beamed and said dreamily, "Eddie. When are you going to ask me over to your house? I want to meet him. And now, icing on the cake, you know Smiles Smythe. Maybe I could come with you to church, too.

"But first things first. When are you bringing me home to meet your brother?"

Theta didn't know what to say, having never had a friend before, let alone imagined bringing a classmate to any of the rented houses that she considered more shelters than homes. It was impossible to think of inviting Sue to this latest one with its stained newspaper wall coverings and outdated outhouse far down a weedy path toward the alley.

While Camille and Marlene often went to other girls' homes to play, they'd never, now that Theta thought about it, ever brought a friend to any of the myriad rental houses they'd occupied. At this moment, in the cavernous assembly hall filled with hundreds of laughing adolescents, she suddenly realized why.

She stammered, "Eddie's gone most all the time, Sue. I'll find out when he'll be home and have you over."

This was a complication she hadn't considered. Until Sue's

self-invitation, it hadn't occurred to her, since neither Camille nor Marlene brought any of their friends to the house, that it was something friends did. The suggestion that she might also invite someone to church was novel as well, although not quite as inconceivable. Not at all. While the thought of introducing a friend to her intimidating mother elicited stomach-wrenching panic, the idea that she might bring Sue to Trinity was truly inviting.

She did love Mrs. Dugranut, her Sunday school teacher. The ancient woman made Sunday school so interesting with the character cutouts she placed on the faded blue felt board during story time that Theta forgot all about her teacher's perpetually shaking head. She forgot that the people in those stories lived thousands of years ago in a land thousands of miles across the globe. She forgot for a wonderful hour every Sunday morning the responsibilities at home that weighed on her shoulders like an uneven yoke.

Eventually, she forgot why she'd come to Trinity in the first place.

Smiles was finishing his speech when Theta realized she hadn't heard any of it, she'd been so wrapped up in her own thoughts. Keeping Sue from her house, inviting Sue to church, the felt-backed Bible characters welcoming her into their world every Sunday.

"Sure, Sue. If you want to go to church, I'll meet you there. It's in Fairview, closer to your house, so there's no reason for you to come all the way over to mine first."

"Sure!"

Chapter Ten

1939

Her Story

Theta could tell they were in for another steamy day when the morning fog shrouding the mountainside didn't dissipate by midmorning. It was still ominously enveloping tree trunks and hovering over the tall jimsonweed along the lane when she and Junior went for the morning mail at ten o'clock. Theta lightly caressed the prickly leaves with delicate fingertips as if the dew were soft and sound as cotton.

"Careful," Junior warned. "That stink weed's poison. Don't put yer fingers in yer mouth."

Theta sighed. She no longer relished summers with her hill cousins, though she adored them. Carefree summers of play had become, at May Nelle's insistence, continuances of her life at home where she was confined to chores and her mother's constant vigil. Worse. This past year she'd achieved some independence from her mother.

She'd been babysitting her brother Matt's two daughters after school and weekends since he'd gotten his wife Judy on with him at the Belden wire factory the previous fall. Staying alone with her nieces was to Theta akin to, as well as exciting as, being Frances Farmer on Broadway. And not just acting as she entered the stage of her brother's Baxter Street double, but also writing and producing as well.

Most important, she was the director in that babysitting scenario.

Her routine was to walk her charges home from their elementary school then after a quick snack send them to play in their upstairs room as she read with rare freedom on Matt's front room davenport. After a few chapters, Theta laid aside her book to set the girls to chores. She chattered to them animatedly. Something her own siblings would be surprised to know.

"You two take rags and dust every stick of furniture in this parlor," she instructed her nieces. "I'll sit here by the window and watch to make sure you do it right. I can teach you best by letting you do it yourselves. Hurry up. Don't forget I want those spindle legs wiped."

She concocted what she thought to be a sophisticated monologue as her brother's daughters went along, addressing the little girls as if they were supporting characters important only as they related to her. "I've been reading this tome. It's a book you may want to read when you're an adult like me. It's quite informative. I know you're impressed that I'm reading well beyond my grade. Everyone is.

"Be careful dusting around that lamp; that's not how *I'd* do it. Hurry up, I must get ready to go to a party with my friends. I have a new dress to wear, you know."

Ignoring her nieces' perplexed glances, Theta continued, "I'll let you do my hair when you finish. I'll just sit here in this easy chair by the window and let you brush it. You have nothing important to do. Stop talking. You can't work and talk at the same time."

She pinched the bridge of her nose between her index finger and thumb. "See now, you've given me a headache with all your chatter. Hush now. You've nothing anyone needs to hear anyway.

"Oh, for heaven's sake, you've dusted those end tables wrong," she sighed. "That's not how *I'd* do it."

Theta wrestled with a nagging thought: She could gently encourage her nieces as she so often wished her mother would her, demonstrating fondness and approval. She knew she had that choice. But another nagging thought overruled, this one an echo. *"I don't get treated like that, so why should they?"*

When the girls were playing in Matt's back yard, as Theta instructed every afternoon so she could listen uninterrupted to Scattergood Baines, she talked back to the Zenith. When she sent them up for a nap before supper, she talked aloud to herself as she purposely went about making the family's evening meal. Even though she took her own supper at home, she thrilled to root around Judy's ample pantry and cupboards to make up recipes as fantastic as her imaginary conversations.

Sometimes, after she'd set the girls to work on unnecessary, tedious tasks like picking specks of lint from Judy's many throw rugs, she used Matt's telephone to gossip with Sue. Having a telephone, even one shared with three parties, was an extravagance beyond Theta's reach or daydreams. She'd worked for her brother nearly two weeks before she asked him, hoping to sound fascinated but not too interested, if he were charged by the call or minute. After Matt explained that unlike other utilities, General Telephone charged a flat monthly fee for local service, she dialed Sue as soon as Matt and Judy left for work.

Even then, she whispered into the dimpled mouthpiece as though at any moment she risked certain discovery.

Saturdays, when Judy and Matt worked half days, were her favorite mornings to play at babysitting. Theta began baking cookies as soon as she saw their late-model Durant turn the corner. It was her chance to bake any kind she wanted, promising the girls, "If you stay in your room and play quietly, you can eat one burnt or misshapen one."

She lined flawless golden-brown cookies on waxed paper in precision rows to cool, gobbling with sacrificial resignation any strays that didn't fit her exacting numerical pattern. Six cookies lined ruler-straight horizontally, six lines vertically on a sheet of waxed paper carefully cut from the roll. She'd be able to tell at a glance if her nieces sneaked even one while her back was turned.

After allowing her nieces their defective treats and putting them down for a late morning nap, she'd take a cup of tea and a few of the stray cookies on one of Judy's prized Noritake dessert plates to the front room. There she daintily tucked her feet under her fanny on the davenport to read in glorious solitude until she saw Matt's Durant pull to the curb shortly after noon.

She'd been earning three dollars a week, which she dutifully handed over to her mother. She thought with hope born of unreasonable reason that this summer May Nelle would allow her to stay in Richmond since she was earning a contributing wage. After all, subsidizing the household treasury seemed to be the most important criteria when May Nelle told Peter that she expected him to live at home to support the family until Camille graduated from high school. At that time, Camille was expected to live at home while maintaining the sugar bowl bank until Marlene got her diploma.

This summer, Eddie successfully convinced their mother that he was old enough to stay alone with Peter. Theta naturally surmised that she could as well. After all, she thought, if her brother could stay home because he played baseball, she certainly could forego the annual Kentucky visit since she was bringing home three precious dollars every week. Probably more since she'd be babysitting all day now that school was out. It made perfect sense.

Though, as usual, she didn't explain her decision, May Nelle must have witnessed with chagrin her youngest daughter's growing independence. Theta imagined with surety born of experience that her mother had weighed her long-term plan against the short-term income.

"Theta won't be able to babysit your girls for the summer," May Nelle told Matt.

Theta was crushed that her mother could be so unreasonable, even with the surefire knowledge that there was quite a bit of selfish reason behind May Nelle's decision.

Matt came back at their mother with, "I'll give her room and board in addition to her wage while you visit kin in Kentucky. Judy and I will keep a good eye on her."

Theta was amazed, wondering if she'd heard him correctly. She'd impulsively and uncharacteristically wrapped her arms around Matt's neck, wiping rebellious tears on his shirt as she hugged her gratitude. Though she could think of no conceivable reason her mother would object, Theta had correctly anticipated that May Nelle would automatically shoot down this novel idea.

She'd thought out all the compelling and rational arguments that supported her belief that Matt's offer was in the best interest of everyone all around. Next, she'd arranged these persuasive points in the order to best present to her mother; had rehearsed them until she was sure May Nelle couldn't possibly refuse. How in the world could she when it was all so logical?

But she did. Theta then resorted to begging, something that surprised her even as she did it. She repeatedly cited what she considered her most convincing argument. "My earnings will bolster our financial security."

May Nelle hadn't even allowed the slightest hope with her usual "We'll see." She simply pressed her lips in the familiar firm, tight line. "Put together the sack of clothes you'll need for the farm. And stop giving me so much trouble.

"Why can't you be more like Camille?"

Theta grabbed hold of the jimsonweed's thorny stalk and

yanked. It was unyielding. *Like Mom.*

"No kiddin', Theta. Y'all better not put that hand in yer mouth," Junior warned again. "You'll get poisoned to death."

Theta swiped her hand against her skirt. "I wouldn't care if I did."

Junior dug both hands into his overall pockets and concentrated on kicking pebbles from the worn tracks in the lane. Theta sighed and shuffled through the envelopes they'd taken from the rusted mailbox perched atop the leaning fence pole. A postcard fluttered to the ground.

"Looky here," Junior said. "Somebody's gone to the beach and sent us a card!"

Theta watched him with disinterest as he bent to retrieve it. Then she saw the picture in his hand. An oil painted photograph of a row of colorful umbrellas parallel to a blue ocean with white capped waves tumbling onto a sandy beach. Gold italic lettering in the upper left corner of the varnished card identified the scene: Virginia Beach, Virginia.

"This is for me!" she cried, suddenly animated.

Junior didn't dispute her, but readily gave up the card as she snatched it from his dusty hand and wiped it clean on her skirt. He leaned his head to peer over her shoulder as she read. "Who's it from?"

"My girlfriend, Sue. She's my best friend. She went with her family to Virginia Beach. Oh, can you just imagine, Junior? They went to Virginia Beach!"

"Can I see? What'd she say?"

Having read it to herself almost twice already, Theta showed the photograph on the front to Junior. She turned the card over to read aloud.

"Dear Theta, How are you? I am fine and having a good time. There is a boardwalk here with a carasel and a ferrus

wheel and I won a cupie doll throwing darts at balloons. Every day we go to the beach. See me under the red one? Ha, ha! Hope you are having fun too. Suzy Q."

Theta turned the card over to study the photograph of the umbrella-lined beach and rhythmic ocean. "I guess the boardwalk is over this way," she said, angling the card as if the promenade might come into view.

"Yeah," Junior agreed. "I wonder if they got one of them diving horses."

"Of course they do!" Theta said with authority. "And a lady rides it down, too. I'll bet."

She continued to examine the card, placing within the picture an imagined scene. "I'm going there. Just as soon as I graduate from college and have a job. I'll have a real savings account and every year I'll go on a vacation. Wherever I want. But every other year I'll go to Virginia Beach no matter what. One year, say, the Grand Canyon, the year after that the beach, and the year after that maybe Niagara Falls, and then the beach again. And then . . ."

Still staring at the card, her voice trailed off. She smiled, sure of her plan, sure of her future beneath a red umbrella.

"I'd come with ya," Junior said, "but I've gotta work summertimes. Next year I'm gonna start helping with the tabacca crops. It'll just be winters I can go travel around, so I guess I caint go to Virginia Beach. Florida. That's where I'm goin'. Maybe you can wait an' go to Miama with me sometimes in the winter."

Theta nodded. "On the years I don't go to Virginia Beach, of course."

After dinner, she helped Aunt Shirlee wash up the dishes as her mother supervised from a sturdy rocker near the hearth. Her cousins had leapt from the table to resume play in the cool of the woods, but this was the second year that Theta had been required to stay near her mother helping with whatever chores Aunt Shirlee reluctantly relegated at May Nelle's direction.

Wiping her hands on her starched apron, Shirlee nodded toward the table that'd been rid of everything but thick slices of yeast bread. "Theta-hon, crumble that in a bowl, then take it on out behind the barn to the geese. Stay out there an' make sure none of 'em git choked on it."

Standing between the girl and her mother, her back a thick curtain against May Nelle's scrutiny, Shirlee added with a wink, "You hear? Don't rush 'em with it. Them silly geese'll choke to death. Spread it slow like ya got all day. Hear now?"

The wooden bowl was shallow and wide, heavier than it appeared. Theta balanced it on her hip as she blindly walked down the worn path, reviewing with dreaming eyes the sandy scene captured on the thatched linen postcard.

In a slip of shade just on the other side of the barn was a round galvanized trough, knee-deep with rainwater. The milk cow stood lazily chewing its cud, pausing now and then for a drink. Ignoring Bossie's disinterested gaze, Theta tucked the card in her pocket and began tossing palmfuls of bread bits to the geese, careful to throw it within the boundaries of the barn's shade. Even so, some landed in the trough. A gander extended his neck slightly above the water but was unable to scoop up the soggy scrap.

Theta leaned over the tub, still balancing the bowl on her hip. Raising one leg behind her for balance, she used her hand like a paddle to move the bread to the gander. The waterlogged pieces simply bobbed. She pushed more vigorously and the bread began to float toward the outer ridge of the tank, but so slowly it threatened to sink. Theta set the wooden bowl at her bare feet and, using her stomach to brace against the trough's rim, agitated the cool water with both hands.

The bread violently washed toward the goose along with a generous splash that landed full on the gander's lowered head. Startled, it reared back with an indignant squawk that roused the other geese from their dusty peckings perilously near Bossie's hooves.

Laughing, Theta splashed the gander again. It raised to a piqued height, flapped its wings, and hollered as if demanding she stop her nonsense and get on with the business of feeding him his dinner. Theta obliged, delighted. The gander danced from toe to toe. Abandoning their lunches, a dozen geese waddled to the galvanized tank and joined in the gander's jitterbug. Bossie blinked her milk ball eyes, an audience to the joy on one side of the trough and raucous commotion on the other.

Theta tucked her skirt into her waistband and stepped into the pool. The geese ran in zany patterns of crazy eights as she scooped water with both hands to splash over them. They honked and danced under the shower, outraged or elated, she couldn't tell which. Theta's arms were windmills at her sides, powered by her laughter, gaining momentum until she whooped happiness under the refreshing spray.

Chapter Eleven

1939

His Story

Jacky couldn't stand to go. She refused to go. Didn't even want to think of the beating her beautiful son may be taking over in Muncie at the Golden Gloves boxing tournament. *And, oh! His gorgeous teeth!* The truth was, Jacky could think of little else as she waited for the phone to ring signaling the end of Smiles' bout. Then she would sigh a prayer of gratitude and pray anew that this was his last fight. Keeping vigil on a stainless-steel kitchen chair pulled close to the telephone stand in the dark hallway, Jacky clasped and unclasped her hands.

Again tonight, though, Smiles' pearly whites had remained intact. Many of his opponents grimaced threateningly through uneven, or more often than not, missing teeth. The one he'd faced tonight had only one broken front tooth, fully vulnerable as the boy pumped his gloved hands in front of his chest. Smiles peered at him with lively azure eyes over the boxing glove protecting his nose. The other glove hid his grin. Disarmed by Smiles' unusual demeanor, the belt-holder had missed the jab to his jaw that sent his head reeling. It was the beginning of his downfall. Before the reigning champ knew it, he was prone on the mat, the referee counting the end to his rule.

The phone hadn't finished its first ring before Jacky pounced on the receiver. She told the operator she'd accept the long-distance charge then held her breath until she heard Smiles' distant laugh. "Mother? You're talking to the Golden Gloves middleweight champion of the state of Indiana! And I still got all my teeth."

Smiles' next call was to his grandmother, who'd been glued to her Philco since early afternoon afraid she'd miss WKBV's broadcasting of the event. She wanted Gordon to drive her to Muncie, but he refused. He wasn't going to "sit on them hard bleachers all night while she made a darn fool of herself yellin' and carryin' on, embarrassin' the boy." So, she commandeered the front room radio, sitting as close as she could to its dinner plate speaker, even when Gordon complained he wanted supper on the table.

"If you'd a-taken me to Muncie," she doled out with crisp reckoning as she remained seated beside the Philco, "you coulda had a weenie at the coliseum. But no, you didn't want to make the drive. You was just too stingy. So you're a-going to have to make a sandwich for your own self."

"Well, turn up the radio then, so I can hear it in the kitchen," Gordon said, unable to hide his grin behind the gruff words.

When Smiles' match finally came over the airwaves, Mildred had barely been able to keep her seat on the edge of the Broyhill. She bounced on its tufted cushion with each jab, weave and duck reported from the arena forty-five twisting and turning miles to the northwest. Gordon, too, had been reenacting with jerking shadowboxing every crackling description of his grandson's movements in the Golden Gloves ring.

Both were exhausted by the end of the bout, though it had lasted a mere three rounds. They were toasting their grandson's victory with glasses of cold, sudsy Hudepohl beer when the telephone rang. Gordon knew the call was hers and stepped aside as Mildred rushed to the telephone.

"Smiles?" she crowed without preface, frowning with impatience. ". . . Of course we'll accept charges! . . . Oh, Smiles, we know! We was listening the whole time and oh how I wish we coulda been there! . . . He did? . . . You did? . . . Well, you've always been a good sport. Did you open your present? . . . It fits okay? . . . We're mighty proud of you, honey . . . Yes, he's here, but we know you got to go . . . Yes, I'll tell him."

Smiles turned from the pay phone, brushing hair darkly wet and curly with sweat from his forehead. His smile broadened at the sight of his high school gym teacher. "Coach! What're you doing here?"

"Well, I didn't want to miss your fight," Dick Tiernan said, ignoring the perspiration staining Smiles' new satin robe to put an arm around his shoulders. "That's the kind of grit I like to see. Now, you take that same attitude to the football field next week, inspire the rest of the fellas, and we're going to have another winning season."

"You bet!"

"Practice starts Monday. But right now, you enjoy this moment."

Eying the robe, already embroidered with the middleweight title below Miles' nickname, Mr. Tiernan chuckled and shook his head. "Mom?"

Smiles looked down at the gold cursive carefully stitched on the maroon mantle's left breast. "How'd you know?"

"I don't know another woman as sure of anyone as that grandmother of yours is of you. She probably had that thing made the first time you put on the gloves back in '33."

"Probably did," Smiles agreed, swiping his forearm above his grin.

"Do me a favor," the handsome, young coach implored with pseudo seriousness. "Tell her to at least let us get halfway through the season before inviting the entire team to her back yard for a state finals picnic."

He patted Smiles on the back, shook his hand, then turned to go. As he passed a line of spent boxers waiting to use the pay phone, he called over his shoulder, "But tell her I want those deviled eggs with the horseradish in 'em again this year."

All the ride home along pitch dark Route 35, Smiles couldn't stop thinking about the football coach and how he'd come to watch his match even though he often said the ring interfered with the gridiron. He turned to Louie in the back seat. "You see Mr. Tiernan?"

"Naw. He there?"

"Yeah. Came back to the dressing rooms after my fight. Drove all the way to Muncie to cheer us guys on. Imagine that."

It was past midnight by the time their trainer dropped off Smiles and Louie in their Fairview neighborhood. Most of the houses lining Butler Street resembled tombstones, straight and narrow, gray in the light of the waning moon. Darkened windows were epithets to sleeping occupants within. But a light still burned in the Smythe's house.

"Your mother waitin' up for ya," Louie stated.

"No. It's Dad. Mother's awake upstairs, you can bet. But it's always Dad who sits up for me downstairs. He likes the blow-by-blow."

Tightening stomach muscles made Smiles feel queasy. He also knew that the longer his father waited up for him, the more likely he'd be to take a drink. Or two. "Well, see ya. G'night."

Smiles hustled up the front steps, taking two at a time until he reached the wooden porch that ran along the side of the house. Only then did he hear the shouting. It was the slurred cursings of his father. Smiles stopped and leaned against the door, closing his eyes against the scene he knew was on the other side. He felt nausea rise to his throat. A too familiar sensation these days.

"Dad!" he called, opening the door, hoping to turn attention and mood.

But the shouting didn't cease. Smiles crossed through the front room into the dining room. He saw Porter in the kitchen shouting at someone just out of sight. Smiles hurried past the cherry dining table, pushing away an overturned chair. He looked to the table and saw on its side a clear bottle whose hundred-ninety proof contents he knew had come from that Nola woman's still down in Happy Hollow. From the corner of his eye he saw his dad lunge past the doorway. Then he heard his mother's painful gasp.

"No!" Smiles shouted, bursting into the kitchen. Porter's hand was a vise around the reddening flesh of Jacky's wrist. She turned pooling eyes from her husband to her son, embarrassment overshadowing her fear.

Smiles grabbed his father's shoulder. "Leave go!"

And with the swiftness of one whose only thought is for his mother, Smiles spun his father around and struck him with a balled-fist uppercut across the jaw that sent Porter's head springing backward like a jack-in-the-box. Smiles had never hit anyone outside the ring. Had never so much as talked back to his father. The two faced each other with identical stunned expressions. Then both began to weep.

With one blow Smiles had ended Porter's drinking and accompanying abuse.

Chapter Twelve

1940

His Story

"Sure, Pop," Smiles said, pressing the unforgiving black telephone receiver uncomfortably against his shoulder and right ear. With some effort he shimmied open the drawer of the end table. "Tell me again the date. Is it a weeknight or a weekend? I have basketball practice every day after school, and we always have a game on the weekend; usually on Friday night but sometimes on Saturday."

He took a scrap of paper from the drawer and after some rummaging, found a stub of a pencil. "Okay. What's the date and time?"

His grandfather, the Grand Noble Officer in the local branch of the Independent Order of Odd Fellows, ignored the question. "You know the Rebekah lodge is co-sponsoring the Christmas party, don't ya, son? So Mom would be tickled pink if you played Santy Claus again this year. You'd make her day."

"You made my day by asking me again, Pop. It's fun and I'm glad you thought I did okay last year. I just have to make sure . . ."

"Them kids liked how you knew their moms and dads and such, called 'em by name. Darned if it didn't make 'em believe you really are Santy! Eyes as big as dollars."

As it turned out, neither Smiles nor his grandfather needed to worry about Santa Claus being able or willing to show up. The Odd Fellow's 1940 Christmas party for the children and grandchildren of lodge members was held on a Tuesday evening, the seventeenth of December.

Smiles hurried from the Civic Hall gym to the locker room

following varsity basketball practice. He'd stuffed the red flannel suit Mom had made him last year into his locker, ignoring jeers from teammates. It'd be worse, he knew, when he actually put the thing on after his shower.

He thanked his lucky stars Mr. Tiernan had offered him a ride to the lodge, located above Davis-Jenkins' jewelry store on the busiest corner of Main Street. This way he could dress ahead of time, right down to the white beard his mother had fashioned from rolled cotton. The little kids wouldn't see him come in and maybe figure out it was him under the get-up when he emerged from changing in the men's restroom at the IOOF dressed in the red suit.

He hadn't figured, though, on the line of children and families climbing the dark stairs around the corner from Davis-Jenkins to the building's second-floor lodge. The ones still outside saw him, incognito, emerge from Tiernan's 1937 Chevrolet Master Deluxe. But it didn't matter that he wasn't stepping from a reindeer-led sleigh. There was a chorus of "Santa Claus!" that greeted then preceded him up the wooden steps.

"Ho, ho, ho!" he bellowed, sounding as jolly as he could under the circumstances, crushed from behind, his progress impeded as the deafening reception erupted and echoed up the enclosed staircase.

A young boy, blind since birth, clinging to his mother's arm, tugged at her coat sleeve. She leaned down. He whispered conspiratorially, "Smiles is here!"

"Oh, no," she said. "It's Santa Claus."

"Mommy," the child chided, "don't you think I know Smiles' voice?"

Somehow Smiles worked his way up the stairs to lead excited children and delighted adults into the grand hall. To him, it seemed as vast as the new high school's Civic Hall gymnasium. In fact, it looked almost like it, with gleaming waxed oak floorboards empty of furniture. All the Odd Fellows' elevated degree seats, now fronted by metal folding chairs, lined three walls like spectator grandstands. Instead of a goal and backboard at one end of the court was an intricately carved throne usually reserved for, as Louie often laughingly put it when he'd seen Smiles' grandfather leaving for a meeting in his flashy Odd Fellows uniform, the "Wizard of Odds."

A bulging, green-dyed flour sack had been set against the garlanded Grand Nobel's prestigious seat. Inside were presents brought the week before by the families of children who were attending tonight's holiday gala. The Rebekah auxiliary had spent a happy evening in the back room kitchen wrapping each gift as their husbands conducted their secret meeting. Smiles was certain it had been Mildreds's idea for the women to do the wrapping so each toy appeared identical as it was pulled by Smiles from the bag.

"C'mon, boys and girls!" the Yuletide Pied Piper said, beckoning youngsters with a wave of his arm to follow him. "Let's see what Santy's elves have left for you!"

As if choreographed, the children, with toddlers in front, gathered in a semi-circle in front of the transformed throne. They lowered themselves in unison to sit cross-legged, chins pointed in anticipation toward Santa's gaudy seat.

Smiles faced his audience, sitting with hands on knees. "Well, let's see . . ." he leaned toward the bag of gifts then stopped, cocking his head and slowly rolling his eyes to the pressed tin ceiling. "Do you hear that? Why, it's Rudolph!"

A hundred sets of peepers looked upward, as if they could see through to the peaked roof where surely balanced Santa's red-nosed reindeer. "Yes! Yes!" most of them cried, some of them pointing. "I hear him!"

"Who brought a treat for Rudolph?"

More hands than Smiles would have thought shot into the air above carefully coiffed heads. Frantically waving vegetables varying from carrots to rutabagas, kids wanted Santa Claus to know they remembered his request from the year before.

"Okay. If you have a treat for Rudolph, you can bring it up when I call your name. But first, who knows whose birthday it is?"

More enthusiastic waving of hands amid shouts. "Jesus'!"

Nodding, Smiles put an index finger to one side of his nose, just as he imagined St. Nicholas did when Jacky read the Christmas poem to him and his sisters. "And you know that's why we give and get gifts at Christmastime, don't you? Because the three kings brought gifts to the baby Jesus. You know who else came to the stable?"

Eyes wide, Smiles' rapt audience shook their heads.

"The humble shepherds came to see baby Jesus, too. They knelt before Him, leaning on their staffs."

Smiles lifted a present from the cotton sack. Tied into the paper curling ribbon, as into all the bows, was a red-and-white striped candy cane. "So now you know why Christmas peppermint sticks are shaped like this. It's curved just like the shepherds' hooks."

Smiles lowered his voice to almost a whisper. "Kings and paupers alike came to the stable to worship baby Jesus. That's why the elves tied candy canes into the ribbons of these gifts: to celebrate Christ's love for each one of you. He loves us no matter who we are or our station in life."

A hundred small heads nodded. Smiles saw Mildred nod, too, caught up in Santa Claus' tale as if she herself hadn't told her grandson these same lessons. It was with a start she remembered that beneath the costume, sincerity, and wisdom was Smiles, barely eighteen years old.

With a grin, Smiles silently read the card attached to the present in his hand. He pointed to the blind boy near the back of the crowd. "Oh, ho, ho, ho! This is a very special toy made by my elves just for little Tommy. Oh, I remember when your mother was your age. Ho, ho, ho. She wanted a doll baby. Isn't that right, Rachel?"

He looked toward Tommy's mother, who vigorously nodded, to the enchantment of the rest of the crowd. She guided her son to Santa. As Smiles leaned forward to place the gift in the boy's hand, Tommy cupped his other palm to his mouth. He whispered conspiratorially into the ear supporting the cotton beard, "Thank you, Smiles.

"And don't worry. Your secret's safe with me."

Chapter Thirteen

1940

Her Story

The week after Christmas, despite the bitter chill, Theta crawled into the drafty cubby hole off her sisters' bedroom amid white blouses and scant skirts dangling from wire hangers. It was the only place in her mother's house she could disappear with a book for an uninterrupted hour. She snuggled to the bridge of her nose under several quilts, a knitted toboggan covering her head, gloved hands shivering slightly as they gripped the spine of the Marjorie Rawlings novel she'd read several times before.

She carefully positioned a flashlight so its beam would fall only on the book and not be visible through the crack of the miniature attic door. If anyone knew she was there, she'd have no peace. Often, in this private library, she could hear her mother calling from downstairs. Later she would say she'd been next door helping with Matt's children. Desperation had made her a clever and easy liar.

But it wasn't her mother's harsh voice she heard as she opened the book, it was Camille's purr. And someone else's. Theta slowly lowered *The Yearling,* afraid a rustling page would give her away. The voices came nearer until the shuffling sounds of soft footsteps joined the whispers. The bedroom door closed with a click rather than a bang. Bed springs rasped. Theta's heart sank; she was trapped. And evidently by ones as intent on privacy as she.

"What can I do?" It was a desperate plea, evidenced by the rising, protracted final syllable.

"Let me think." That was Camille. "Are you sure this means

84

anything?"

"I told you it does!" The second voice was passionate though hushed. Hissing with unchecked contempt. "He gave her a purse for Christmas. Didn't even hide it from me. And he didn't get me anything! Not a thing! And this morning he tells me he's going out of town for a few days."

There were building wails, suddenly muffled.

"Shh!" Camille's voice again. "If Mom hears us, she'll be up here in a flash to find out what's going on. No one can know. We have to be very discreet until we figure something out. If Mom finds out, it will kill her. And she'll kill Mark, too!"

Mark? Then the other voice must belong to her brother's wife Georgeanne, uncharacteristic restraint disguising her usual boisterous peal. Theta leaned toward the closed door, her eyes searching the darkness of the slanted ceiling as she strained to hear what would come next.

"Maybe he's going on a business trip," Camille continued hopefully.

Georgeanne, sounding miffed and impatient with her sister-in-law, said, "He is a line machinist, Camille."

There was a brief silence. "Besides, he's not making a secret of it. He practically flaunts her in my face. First with the purse. Then he doesn't give me anything for Christmas. And now this morning he announces he's taking a trip and won't be back until Thursday. You know what that means? He's taking her on a vacation!"

Theta strained to make out Georgeanne's anguished words through her sister-in-law's hiccuping sobs, but could hear only muffled, indecipherable whispers. What was Camille saying? Was it she or Georgeanne who was whispering now?

Then she clearly heard her sister's voice. "When did you first suspect?"

"Not 'til he bought that purse. I thought it was for me, but he said he was giving it to Harriett Campbell down at the Lamplight."

Harriett Campbell! Theta nearly blurted her surprise before clasping a gloved hand to her blanketed mouth. Eyes wide with disbelief, Theta pictured the flirtatious waitress who famously rubbed her voluminous breasts against married men's shoulders as she leaned over their backs while precariously balancing blue plate specials on a tray with one flat hand.

Her mother really would kill Mark. Just with her eyes.

"To tell the truth," Georgeanne continued, "even then I didn't think a whole lot about it on account of he'd been talking about her a lot. We laughed about how she could get them old baldies to blush then leave big tips. We thought she was funny. I knew how much he liked her—his favorite waitress and all.

"She was my favorite waitress, too," she continued with disgust. "It didn't even register he was spending a lot of time down there without me. He brought home our supper from there a lot, it being on the way from the Crosley and all, and me working late most days. But when he didn't get me anything for Christmas it hit me like a ton of bricks."

Theta heard her blow her nose; a trumpeting blast followed by a lengthy void.

Georgeanne finally said, through lingering sniffles, "I'd have to be a real dope to not know something's up after he had the time to go buy a purse for a dumb old waitress but not a solitary thing for his own wife."

"What'd you do when you figured it out?"

"Well, at first I was mad. We had a big fight and he left and didn't come home 'til the next day."

"He was gone on Christmas?" Camille whispered, emphasizing the holiday as if Georgeanne had purposely embellished Mark's iniquity.

There was a pause and Theta imagined her sister's look of consternation as she sized up the situation. Then, "That's bad. Really bad. Christmas day! Did he tell you where he went?"

"He didn't have to. When we were fighting, he acted like Harriett was the one wronged. He defended her. To me!"

"And now he's going away over New Years?" Camille said.

"I'm just so scared he's going away forever!" There were shrill cries, suddenly muffled again. Theta envisioned Camille's hand pressing against their sister-in-law's gaping mouth. Then more hiccupping.

"I'll die if he leaves me, Camille. What can I do?" Georgeanne wailed the last, warbling word.

Theta, motionless in the darkness of both the attic and her imaginings, knew exactly what she'd do. Any husband of hers would be lucky to get out of the house alive. But evidently the answer didn't come so handily in the bedroom. There were only hiccups amid stifled sobs for what seemed an eternity.

Finally Camille had an idea. "I know. I know how you can make sure Mark stays with you."

A suspenseful moment preceded the pronouncement. "You need to have a baby."

The hoarse sobbing stopped abruptly. Theta heard the rusty bedsprings protest as a weight lifted from the mattress. Georgeanne must've stood up.

"Get pregnant?" Her sister-in-law's voice was incredulous as if Camille had suggested she procreate with Germany's Adolph Hitler. Then she sounded offended, piqued. "Do you know how hard I've had to work to get where I am? How much influence I've finally got over at the Sar Serie? Why, now that I'm off the line, now I'm secretary to the foreman, some of 'em listen to me. I have their ears, Camille!"

Theta, musing that of all people, Georgeanne would surely correctly and clearly pronounce Bucyrus Erie. She heard the springs again, signaling Camille had also risen. But Georgeanne was on a roll.

"I'm in line to be secretary to some of the men in the office. Me! Name one other woman you know who's gotten this far. At a big company like the Sar Serie. You can't. And I'm not going to give that up. A baby would ruin things!"

"Shh. Sit down," Camille managed to hiss. The rusted springs sinking into themselves groaned more loudly this time. "Mom will know something's going on up here. Listen, Georgeanne, you've got to decide. Mark or your job. If you have a baby, he won't dare leave. But if what you're saying is true, you'd better get pregnant now because it seems to me things are moving pretty fast with that Campbell woman. Mark might ask for a divorce."

There was silence. Then Camille thrust home to win her point. "Or worse."

Theta's mind raced. What could be worse? Camille provided the answer for both her and the stubbornly unconvinced Georgeanne. "Harriett could be the one to get pregnant."

Theta's eyes were wide with bleak visions. It surely would kill her mother. From her station in the overstuffed chair by the front window, May Nelle was an avid spectator. She loved to regale Theta with neighborhood gossip as she oversaw her youngest daughter executing any number of household chores. Now her mother would be on the other end of maliciously delicious tales. Right out of Dante, Theta thought as she heard Camille and Georgeanne leave the bedroom.

Chapter Fourteen

1941

Her Story

Red and yellow tulips drooped along the back fence the day Mark and Georgeanne burst through the kitchen door with their surprising news. May Nelle, supervising Theta from the corner rocker, screamed happiness, clapped her hands, and motioned with open arms for the couple to cross the kitchen to receive her innocent hugs. Marlene paused with fork halfway to her open mouth. She looked stunned by the happy news so late into her brother Mark's marriage. Camille purposely set her coffee cup on a chipped saucer as she struggled to constrain a victorious, knowing grin.

Theta wiped a dinner dish with a ragged but fresh linen towel. She leaned close to Camille and said the words she'd been rehearsing since that cold December afternoon: "You were right. Looks like he's going to stay."

Two months later, Theta ripped open a case of Heinz catsup like a kid at Christmas. Indeed, this day had been as anticipated as most everyone's favorite holiday. Theta had at last managed to find a way to escape May Nelle's constant grasp. Her unlikely asylum was to be found inside the wooden concessions stand at Springwood Lake. Two simple sentences whispered into Camille's ear had, as she'd known they would, cleared the way.

Inside the cardboard case was the last of the gallon catsup jugs she'd been carefully arranging like Beefeaters on the wooden shelves lining the back wall of the refreshment stand. Gallon jars of yellow mustard stood at attention beside their red counterparts. Completing the inventory on the whitewashed boards were five-pound burlap bags of unpopped corn, quart bottles of cooking oil, and cellophane packages of hot dog buns.

By the light of a single bulb suspended by a cord from a nail in the ceiling, Theta had that morning opened and aligned a dozen small cardboard boxes on the island in the middle of the concession stand. The rough-hewn table, resembling a garage workbench, was home to neat rows of Hershey, Baby Ruth, and a family of Mars candy bars. She'd placed them in alphabetical order, after considering and rejecting placement according to color coordination. On either side of the candy boxes sat the Ritz Theater's old popcorn popper and a hot dog cooker the size of her mother's cathedral Philco.

On an open shelf braced between the island's supports sat a GE Catalin Bakelite radio. Her very own for the summer. No soap operas for her. She liked listening to the Cincinnati Reds on WLW. And that was just what she intended to do, though she anticipated that sunbathers would howl for upbeat big band blasting through loudspeakers connected by long wires to the Catalin.

The popper belched the last of its aromatic popped corn onto the machine's chrome floor, ready to be ladled into paper bags. Wieners were already beginning to sweat on their rotating spikes, and the buns were softening in the steam bin atop the rotisserie. All Theta needed to do now was fill the baseball sized glass condiment jars with relish, mustard and catsup then set them on the narrow serving shelf that would separate her from hungry customers.

Neither nervous nor excited about the lake's opening day, Theta instead was in her element: resplendently in charge.

Theta inspected with a sergeant's frown the boxes of candy bars she'd propped at an angle to display their chocolate and nougat contents. She nodded satisfaction. Not bad for her first stint manning the forest green concessions shack. She unlatched the stand's upper facade, a horizontal barn door that could be propped up like an awning to reveal the refreshments inside.

The miniature barnlike stand sat on the lake's eastern shore near a chicken coop of a bathhouse. Sand was brought in by the truckloads the weekend before every Memorial Day to make a beach fronting the spring-fed swimming hole. The oasis was made complete by two wooden rafts in the lake just beyond the shallows and a cement diving island that served as a border between swimmers and fishermen.

Usually members of the Conservation Club scouted Richmond High School's junior and senior class beauties to recruit sirens to sell fund-raising concessions. The stand had been Camille's domain last year. All summer the hut had been a hive of activity with boys attracted to its manager like bees to a rose. This summer, though, the alluring graduate had taken work on the linen assembly line at the Bucyrus Erie.

At their first-quarter board meeting, the Conservation Club's treasurer had reported that Camille's summer of 1940 had been a record year for concessions, providing the additional revenue to finally build the croquet court they'd been postponing since 1929.

The coming summer, he'd noted in an exultant motion, promised to generate enough profit to at last put lights around the horseshoe court, since the exceptionally striking Camille had said she'd work weekends if they hired her sister to run the stand. There was a swift second and the proposition passed unanimously, many of the men having seen Marlene sunbathe as they made minor repairs to the beach's fence or sound system during their rushed but rewarding lunch hours.

There was some consternation when the sister, unnamed in the club's motion to hire, turned out to be Camille's surprisingly plain sibling Theta. With much vindicating harrumphing, the men had complimented themselves for hiring the girl who had at least some experience in the profitable stand. She was the one, each insisted, they'd meant all along.

When she returned from the Kentucky hills the summer of 1940, Theta had helped Camille pack up the refreshment stand's inventory and close up for the winter. She was offered a dollar to help after Marlene opted to spend the last day at the lake lying on an old quilt, nonchalantly picking sand off her mahogany, baby-oiled arms and legs.

Now Theta returned the newly opened gallon jars of relish, mustard, and catsup to the Kelvinator. She recalled how she'd scrubbed that refrigerator the fall before. It was with harsh detergent in scalding water. As she bent to reach the back of the bottom shelf, she dared not turn her head to identify the bevy of boys flirting with Camille.

As she worked, she mumbled to herself. "I don't care anyway. I'd rather see gleaming enamel emerge from encrusted, unidentifiable splatters."

She had used her thumbnail to chip away the grime. She'd been assigned to clean the hut while Camille hawked half-priced candy and bestowed the last of the hot dogs on favored admirers.

From the corner of her eye Theta had spied muscled lifeguards glean remnants of mustard and catsup from condiment jars so heavily scraped they were translucent. More than a few of those Adonisses had made multiple trips to help deplete the stand's remnants from their own Aphrodite. Someday, Theta had thought as she used a Brillo to shine a refrigerator rack, she'd be the one to dole out favors to whomever she pleased.

And now that day had come. Closing the Kelvinator's door,

she smiled with satisfaction as she surveyed the concession stand. This was her realm. She could decide who got the last Snickers and then bask in admirers' appreciation. Camille's bubbling laughter echoed through the refreshment stand like a ghost, but she didn't care. She was in charge of every inch of the shack, to Marlene's boiling irritation.

The middle Whittle girl had been confident that the prestigious post would be hers after Camille graduated high school and took full-time work, probably in a factory. Instead, she'd been inexplicably betrayed on Theta's behalf. While Marlene watched in open-mouthed disbelief following Mark and Georgeanne's baby announcement, Camille had convinced their mother to allow Theta to stay in town to earn a wage instead of shadowing Aunt Shirlee for yet another summer.

"What are you doing?" Marlene had hissed, grabbing Camille's wrist as the older sister walked into the hallway outside their mother's bedroom. "You promised the concession stand to me."

"Never mind. You don't need to know."

Neither Marlene nor May Nelle discovered the real reason Camille had been so insistent that Theta be allowed to stay home the summer of 1941. They never guessed why Camille had awarded Theta the coveted job at Springwood. It was a mystery May Nelle put out of her head but was burned into Marlene's memory.

Theta knew but would never consciously admit to herself, her mother, or anyone else the inadvertent part she'd played in Camille's sudden change of mind.

After inspecting once again her morning's work making the stand ready for customers, she turned the knob on the GE to Richmond's radio station WKBV. She wasn't thinking about her months-ago remark or Camille's astonished blue eyes. The local news was just about to come on. Theta's mouth pressed into a smug smile. No one here, where she was completely in charge, could dictate what the radio played.

It didn't matter to Theta as she wiped already clean surfaces that the staccato report from the radio was booming over the loudspeakers atop the beach's fence posts. She may be asked to switch to music popular with sunbathers, but only she would make the determination whether or not to move the dial. At home, she may have to endure soap operas preferred by the newly unemployed Georgeanne, but here at Springwood, she was the one in charge. Completely, positively, wonderfully in control.

This is what she was thinking this first day of the season as she moved the freshly filled mustard jar a fraction of an inch to complement the placement of the catsup and relish jars. While straightening the stack of paper napkins and securing them with a smooth round rock, she heard blasting from a dozen loudspeakers over the pristine beach WKBV's lead news story.

"A single-car accident early this morning on Straightline Pike claimed the life of Miss Harriett Campbell of Richmond."

Chapter Fifteen

1941

His Story

Smiles yawned as he peered out over sparkling diamonds bouncing off Springwood Lake. Having just graduated from high school, he thought he could keep his daytime lifeguard job and still work nights at Uncle Marne's neighborhood grocery this summer. He figured it wouldn't take long to restock shelves and mop up.

But he hadn't counted on the boxes and boxes of canned goods to be carried from the cellar before he could stock the shelves. Or having to be back at the grocery at five the next morning to meet the dairyman who brought fresh eggs and milk. All of which had to be carefully placed in the cooler before Smiles could sprint to Mom's for a quick breakfast of pie or tapioca before heading to the lake.

He yawned again, blinking his eyes to focus more clearly on raucous teenagers diving and playing near the cement island where he occupied the wooden lifeguard stand.

Smiles wearily watched pimply adolescents dunk squealing girls and come dangerously close to those willing targets with cannonballs off the wooden rafts. He wondered if he should have taken factory work like the rest of the gang. The weekly pay from his two jobs barely matched just one shift on the line at the Malleable.

The thing was, though, he liked kids. He liked to hear them laugh. Liked to let them bury him in the sand during his breaks and stand on his shoulders as he waded from the beach out to the deep end, throwing them off as he dove to swim to the concrete island. It was as if he were still just a kid himself.

No, he was doing the right thing, he decided; piece work was no match for the payback he got every day from the laughing kids at Springwood Lake.

Mr. Tiernan had tried to talk him into going to college. He'd be a good teacher. A great coach. But Smiles didn't think he was smart enough for that. Before his dad stopped drinking, Porter had often told him he was dumb. So often that Smiles believed him. Besides, except for Eddie Whittle, who'd gotten an athletic scholarship to Ball State Teachers' College, none of Smiles' friends were extending their educations beyond high school.

His eyes shifted to the refreshment stand. Smiles thought he might open a conversation with that shy little sister of Eddie's. Maybe ask her about her brother while putting a nickel down for a 3 Musketeers bar. He'd been trying to think of a reason to talk to her. That'd be a good opener. Then maybe ask her to a movie show. Yeah, why not? He'd do that during his next break.

The sun pressed into Smiles' shoulders, warmed his palomino hair. His eyes drooped. The laughter and screams of delight, mingled with sounds of splashing and the springing diving boards, developed a rhythm. A soothing symphony that seemed to drift into pianissimo. Smiles' eyelids kept time; his head nodded forward and jerked back. The sun blanketed him in its warmth. His thoughts rambled, drifted into the surreal.

Sleep hadn't yet enveloped him before the flowing summer melody became strangely disjointed. Faraway screams of gleeful swimmers neared and intensified. They changed. Smiles was suddenly wide awake. The screams were those of a young girl repeatedly calling a boy's name from one of the diving boards. She was standing precariously on the board's lip. Below her, the water was calm. The girl was calling into the deep, frantically appealing to nothing.

Smiles stood and propelled himself into the lake, his arrow

hands splitting the water. He often launched himself from the wooden lifeguard stand to save someone who'd misjudged the sudden slant of the sandy shore as it became mud on the bowl of the lake floor. In the three summers he'd worked at Springwood, he'd rescued more than a dozen show-offs in trouble beneath the diving boards. He even pulled an unconscious man to safety after he hit his head doing a back flip. But this time Smiles didn't know where the boy was.

The water was murky and dark. Smiles' hands brushed underwater plants. It could be hair. He flipped around and tugged at the waving strands. No, definitely plants. He felt along the bottom of the lake. Nothing but mud. He came up for air and propelled himself back to the depths beside the ragged cement of the diving island. This time his arms made wide butterfly arches as he searched inches above the lake's bed. He turned and cut the sinister water with probing scissor strokes. He tried to gauge how far from the island he was. Above him was the outline of a diving board breaking the sun's eerie glare. Up for air.

Down again, he swam closer to the craggy island base, his hands kneading mud. Suddenly he felt a stinging sensation on his left shoulder. Turning, he felt with his fingertips broken rebar escaping crumbling cement. He squinted upward to be sure he was beneath the board, then swam in wider circles just above the lake's floor, his lungs searing in his chest. He prayed for stamina, knowing the boy was nearly out of time.

And then he felt something. Grabbing hold, he was sure it was a foot.

Smiles pulled the boy to the surface and pushed him onto the island, then heaved himself up, panting. Bending over the prone teenager, Smiles turned him on his stomach and began to push his back and pull his waist. Turning him to his back, Smiles tilted the boy's head, pinched his nostrils, and blew into his mouth. He hooked his hands under the boy's armpits; he pulled his arms forward several times, then was about to repeat his breathing resuscitation when the boy gasped, coughed, gagged, expelled a good deal of slimy water, then gasped again.

Smiles sat back on his heels, his chest heaving. A crowd had gathered. Smiles leaned against the legs of some of the onlookers, closed his eyes and blew relief from billowed cheeks. "Thank you, Jesus."

He carried the revived teen to a rowboat and placed him in the girlfriend's lap. He got into the dingy himself and began to powerfully row, though he was weak and winded. Gratefully relinquishing the boy to ambulance attendants waiting on the beach, Smiles dropped heavily to his knees and leaned into them, gasping gratitude. He knew that his drowsiness could have cost the kid his life.

The next thing he knew, Mr. Rivir was taking his arm and asking about the two parallel inch-long bleeding wounds on his shoulder. Smiles for the first time realized the rebar had sliced his skin and knew their scars would never let him forget this frightening day at Springwood when he'd nearly let a boy drown.

He shrugged off his injury, but not the nagging vision of the unconscious boy lying on the cement island.

The next day he put in for work at the Richmond Iron Works. Like most other core makers in the summer of 1941, Smiles assumed it would be a job he'd hold for the rest of his life.

Chapter Sixteen

Fall 1942

His and Her Story

Light streaming through the stained-glass windows of Trinity Methodist Church cast mesmerizing multicolor shadows over its congregants. Theta sat as close as she could to the far right wall of the top row of the church's balcony without leaning irreverently against it. She turned her eyes from the fantastically hued people below to the young women and few young men filling the five balcony rows in front of her. She knew most of the regulars by the backs of their heads, their haircuts or hats.

Smiles wasn't among them. He, along with his gaggle of friends, had enlisted in the Navy following Pearl Harbor. The last she'd heard, the gang had graduated from the Great Lakes Naval Station near Chicago. Who knew where those ruffians were now? She didn't care, except for one.

He'd habitually sat in the center seat of the balcony's front row surrounded by the usual cast of characters who shadowed him since they were youngsters. Feeling melancholy, Theta turned her attention to the faded red hymnal as the congregation rose to sing one of her favorites.

"A mighty fortress is our God, a bulwark never failing." She didn't take a breath before the next verse as everyone else did. "Our helper He, amid the floor of mortal ills prevailing . . ."

Suddenly aware of an affected baritone squeezing in beside her, she was shocked that a man's beefy hand took hold of her book as if invited to share. Annoyed by the nerve and deep growl of this intruder, she turned a disapproving frown to his earnest face. Smiles! He continued to sing as if he didn't notice her changing scowl or shaking hand. When the hymn was finished, he grinned at her before pushing down his flip seat and settling quietly in to listen to Reverend Stephenson's sermon.

Theta again heard Smiles' exaggerated baritone during the Doxology, signaling an end to the worship service. She was struck by the beauty of his voice and wondered how she could have been so annoyed earlier. Embarrassed to be standing so close to him, she lowered her head, hunched her shoulders, and waited for him to move toward the aisle so she could make her escape.

"Hey, little sister," he said, obviously alluding to Eddie, "I want to ask your advice about something."

Theta couldn't imagine that he was speaking to her. Obviously, she thought, he must be home on leave, had come in late and found that the only available balcony seat was next to her. She glanced toward the steps leading from the front row. Smiles' sisters were among the group, most still teenagers, and nearly all dating their high school sweethearts. As if exiting school and not church, they noisily elbowed their way up the carpeted stairs toward the stairway leading to the main floor. Hailing the tardy Smiles, they beckoned him to follow them outside.

"I'll be along," he said, waving the younger clique to go ahead without him. "Gotta catch up with what Eddie's been up to. Haven't seen him since graduation."

"You want my advice?" Theta asked incredulously, staring at her feet.

"Yeah, it's not something I want to let out. It'll only take a minute."

With the balcony emptied, Smiles indicated the oak flip seats they'd occupied during the service. "Do you have time to sit for a minute?"

"Okay," Theta stammered, wondering why he wanted the

advice of a girl still in high school; someone he barely knew.

Smiles turned to face her. Theta stared straight ahead.

He got right to it. "A fella I worked with at the Malleable asked me to do something I know isn't right. I told him I wouldn't. But now I'm wondering if maybe that was far enough. What he has planned is wrong, and well, I've been kinda bothered about whether or not I should tell somebody. Don't want to be a squealer, but maybe I should stop this thing by telling somebody. Maybe I hafta because now that I know it, I'm involved if it happens. Do you get it?"

Theta turned her eyes but not her face toward Smiles and nodded. His expression indeed revealed the quandary was a heavy one. His interlaced fingers flexed inward then outward. She was surprised to realize he was possibly more nervous than she.

"But maybe even if it happens, it's nothing you should worry about," she ventured. "How bad is it? Against the law or something?"

"Worse than that. It could hurt someone's future, maybe a lot of people's. And in my gut, I'm pretty sure it's against everything that's right about America."

"You can't let it get out, so that's why you're asking me instead of one of your friends? Or even your parents?"

"Well, yeah. It's been hard, though, because I've been going 'round and 'round about what to do all weekend and just can't come to a decision. I don't know if saying no to this thing is enough, but I've never been a squealer. That's why I can't ask anybody that knows the person. And, besides, the guys would say right away that it's wrong to be a stool pigeon. They wouldn't have to think twice about it.

"But when I saw you sitting here, I just sorta felt . . . I knew you'd be the one to ask." He smiled, open and relieved.

Turning toward him, Theta said in a naturally serious tone the truth she knew. "You're an honest person. You've done the right thing to not get involved in something that I gather is dishonest or maybe even illegal. But, Smiles, I don't know if you should tell anybody or not. Can you give me more information?"

He took a deep breath. "It's complicated. I don't think it's anything anybody'd go to jail for or anything. But it's something that could affect a city election. Make it unfair against one of the candidates."

"How so?"

Smiles laid out the plan. The Republicans had a near-monopoly on city affairs, with the mayor, a sure re-election of the city clerk, and all but one district of councilmen having a firm majority on the next city government. It'd be a clean sweep for the GOP if it weren't for Francis Marino, a popular Democrat running in the city's southside Second District.

Smiles had been approached by a middle-aged core maker at a high school football game the night he came home on leave. He was still wearing his enlisted-man's blues.

It'd pay well, the man said, if Smiles would help out a week before the election. Take a couple rolls of dimes and open every newspaper box in town just after they were loaded with the morning paper. He was to take out the newspapers and replace them with flyers making Marino look not only bad, but bad enough to effectively swing the election to his Republican opponent Emmett Haas.

"I know it'd be theft to take the papers," Smiles said. "But replacing them with dirt on Mr. Marino is another can of worms. It's not fair; goes against everything America's about."

Theta processed what she'd just been told. "Every newspaper box in town? Why not in just his district?"

"I don't know. Maybe to influence the whole city, make

news so people will talk and word get around to people who don't buy newspapers from boxes? Can't tell ya 'cause I have no idea."

"Well, it's a good plan. Er, bad plan."

Smiles chuckled.

"It's really not funny," Theta apologized. "I agree with you, it's un-American to mess with an election."

Resisting the urge to take Smiles' hand, she said, "You're smart to not do it. You could be arrested, or at the very least take the fall for somebody who knows he could get in trouble so won't raid those boxes himself."

"Me, smart?" Smiles was genuinely surprised to hear it.

"Yes. You're smart to stay honest. And you're smart because you know if it does happen, someone's going to get the blame. You don't have to tell me, but is it Mr. Haas who's behind it?"

"No. I do know that. The guy who asked me to do it has an uncle who owns a printing company somewhere in the county. Says this is a Republican county and he's not about to let some liberal get a foothold. He says there aren't enough Democrats to get up a game of euchre in this county, and that's the way he means for it to stay."

"Oh. Well, I guess my advice is to be true to your values. You've already declined to be a part of it. Just step back. They may decide it's not a good idea, too, if they don't have anyone to do their dirty work."

Theta hesitated, then said, "If you feel it's wrong to be a squealer, as you put it, then that's legitimate."

Smiles nodded, considering. "It's wrong."

"Then there's your answer."

In late October, Theta read in the morning *Item* that every city newspaper box had been vandalized. Newspapers had been stolen from each one, replaced with flyers making fun of

Republican candidate for Second District councilman, Emmett Haas.

Francis Marino, the article alleged, was the prime suspect.

Theta dropped the newspaper to her lap, confused. Her eyebrows lifted as it dawned upon her that the printer of the flyers was more diabolical than Smiles or she had realized. It wasn't what the flyers said that was meant to influence voters, it was who they thought was behind it.

Theta could imagine the printer's amusement as he, too, read the Republican newspaper publisher's biased editorial implicating Mr. Marino.

The next Tuesday, November 5, Theta grinned to imagine the perpetrator's laughter turning to anger as he read the morning paper. Of all candidates, only one Democrat had been elected in the city of Richmond: Francis Marino. The flyers had been intended to sway the election by making voters furious with the person they thought responsible for the nefarious deed. What the printer of the flyers hadn't counted on was the unblemished reputation of Francis Marino. Voters had not been fooled, except perhaps a little.

To the printer's sure chagrin, they instead blamed the crime on the innocent Haas.

Chapter Seventeen

Summer 1943

His Story

The boxer lying spread eagle in the center of the ring, down for the count, didn't resemble any of the young men Smiles had defeated in his years as a Golden Gloves pugilist. This one was a bona fide contender. This guy had taken on Tony Zale, for crying out loud. Hadn't taken the prize, but still . . .! And now he was out cold, sound as a sleeping baby, from the glove of an amateur. Smiles bounced from one foot to the other, victoriously pumping his fists and flipping perspiration from dark golden ringlets bouncing over his glistening forehead.

Uncle Marne shouted from Smiles' ringside corner to the crowd in general. "Still undefeated! That's my sister's kid. Ain't lost a fight yet, I tell ya!"

Smiles couldn't hear him. He wasn't aware of the roar of hundreds of sailors packed into the Norfolk Naval Yard gymnasium to witness the exhibition between the professional boxer and the Navy's boxing team's champion middleweight. Only the sound of his own incredulous thought rang with a pulsing repeating rhythm in his ears. "A contender, for crying out loud!"

The referee took Smiles' right hand and held it aloft. More deafening cheers from enlisted and commissioned alike. Uncle Marne bolted between the ropes knocking over Smiles' stool and spit bucket, his GOB hat flying off his balding head. He swept his nephew from the referee still declaring him the taker of the bout by a knockout.

And still Smiles couldn't keep his eyes off his battered opponent being dragged to his own corner. "*I just knocked out*

Reuben Shank, who knocked out Sugar Ray Robinson, for crying out loud!" he thought, amazed.

Uncle Marne had him by the waist with both arms, trying in vain to lift him in victory celebration, dancing him in circles. "My sister's kid," he shouted gleefully to the rafters and far corners of the gymnasium.

Smiles spit out his mouth guard, laughed, and patted his uncle on the back with a huge, gloved hand as he pulled away. He walked to Shank's corner where the vanquished fighter slumped on his three-legged stool. His trainer was briskly rubbing his shoulders with a wet and bloody towel.

Smiles extended his glove to the groggy contender but addressed the trainer. "He all right?"

"Sure. I'm all right, kid," the professional mumbled drowsily. "You got one hell of a right."

He turned swollen and bloodshot eyes upward and squinted into the light beyond Smiles' shoulder. "I ain't never gone down like that. Where you been fightin'?"

Smiles shook his head and groaned as if he were the one defeated. "Right here."

The rest of the Fairview gang were the real fighters, on aircraft carriers in the Pacific. They'd all gone as one to enlist in the United States Navy the Monday after Pearl Harbor. Every one of them sailors; even Bud, who lied about his age. The expectation was that they'd stay together. And they did stay together, right up until they left basic training at the Great Lakes Naval Base near Chicago to be assigned different vessels.

But Smiles was sent to Norfolk to join the Navy's boxing team.

The others were separated, too, each one on a different carrier thousands of sea miles apart. As far as Smiles was concerned, though, they were still a singular gang because they were all in the war. He was the only one left behind. Even Mr. Tiernan was serving in the Pacific.

Fighting with the Navy Boxing Team wasn't why he enlisted. With men needed to bring down Hirohito, it was beyond Smiles' understanding how knocking out another United States serviceman in the ring, however entertaining, was in any way knocking Japan's powers out of the water.

"It's the same as the USO, ya see," his Navy boxing trainer had explained. "That's why I'm here at my age. I'm bringin' morale to these brave men and homesick boys. They love a good fight and we're gonna give it to 'em. You and me is as important to this war as any gunner. Any admiral as far as that goes, and don't let nobody tell ya otherwise. Ya think Roosevelt don't know that?"

Unconvinced, Smiles had nodded kindly at the Old Man before attacking the speed bag as if it were the grinning bucktooth caricature of Hirohito. To this day, with an unlikely victory feeding the cacophony of cheers echoing throughout the cavernous gymnasium, he was still unconvinced.

Uncle Marne grabbed Smiles' shoulder, nodding congenially but dismissively in the direction of the revived boxer as he pulled his nephew away. "Head to the showers, kid. We're gonna hit the clubs tonight!"

"Naw," Smiles said. "I'm expected over to the Herts'. June's saving supper for me. Have fun, though."

"You and them do-gooders. You got your own mom and dad at home. What you need these for? I know some young ladies who'd adopt ya all right. And wouldn't be servin' ya no chicken dinner neither, if ya know what I mean." Marne winked and Smiles laughed, neither one understanding the other's choice of R & R. Or how Smiles had landed in the care of Preston and Pearl Hert.

The first weekend in Norfolk, Smiles had found a Methodist church near the base. It was by the grace of God he'd happened to sit next to a middle-aged couple who asked him home to Sunday dinner. As they walked to the couple's Lincoln Continental, they were joined by two animated young women, obviously delighted to have a handsome sailor coming home for their mother's famous roast beef.

Sometimes even Smiles couldn't understand his magnetic attraction to June Hert. She was as different from Smiles' hometown girl as North from South. Grace was quiet, passive. June was a mouthful of toothy laughter, coy. Grace was demure and doled out kisses as if they were purchased with ration stamps. June loved to smooch. Even their appearances were polar. June was, as Marne had once observed, built like a brick barn. Grace was . . . well, was not.

But what Smiles really liked about June was that she always had ideas about where to go and what to do. He never liked it when Grace would slide in beside him in his dad's Oldsmobile and shrug, "I don't care. What do you want to do?" It made him feel flustered, afraid he'd choose something she didn't really like. It was impossible to please someone who never let you know what they wanted. But with June there was never a doubt.

"Get a move on!" she shouted in her sensual Southern drawl as she hurried down her front walk to greet Smiles following his victory over the former contender. "Elbert says there's a record-makin' machine on the Boardwalk! Let's go make us a recordin'."

Standing on her toes to quickly buss Smiles' cheek, she asked rat-a-tat, "Didja win? You don't look like a glove touched you, honey. How's the other guy look? Come on, now, let's get goin' to the beach so we can make us a record!"

They ate cold drumsticks wrapped in waxed paper and drank

iced sweet tea from a thermos as Smiles drove the Herts' Lincoln the twenty miles from Norfolk to Virginia Beach. June's sister Peg and her fiancé Elbert sat huddled in the back seat, riotously imitating June holding up darkly fried chicken legs for Smiles to bite into as he drove.

"Y'all go ahead and laugh," June grinned. "We don't care a bit, do we, honey? We're havin' us a picnic. Y'all go ahead and do whateveh ya'll want back there. If I were you, though, I wouldn't be payin' so much attention to what's goin' on up here. Take another bite, honey."

Smiles leaned in to grab another mouthful of crisp, salty chicken. This was living, he thought, driving the massive luxury car with June nuzzling his neck and feeding him like he was Marc Antony. She tipped the yellow plastic thermos cup to his lips, holding an embroidered linen napkin under his chin.

Trying not to choke while chewing and gulping the sugary Southern iced tea, Smiles leaned his head toward the open driver's-side window. His elbow rested on the door's edge and he steered with the fingertips of his left hand. His right arm extended over the seat's back rest, a muscled pillow for June's temple. He could smell the ocean as they neared the Boardwalk, could hear distant crashing of waves against shore. June kissed the corner of his mouth and carefully rolled her tongue over her lips, tasting the remnants of sweetened Lipton.

Oh yes, this was living!

Sailors packed the Boardwalk, shoulder to shoulder; most with a local girl or two on their arms. They crowded games of skill that took more ability than they possessed in optimistic attempts to win ceramic bulldogs or Kewpie dolls for their dates. The night was balmy and many of the girls had removed their stockings to stuff into shoes dangling from hands. These were the girls who would later steer their swabs away from the marquee lights of the Boardwalk to the beach where warm sand provided a cushion for seduction.

June, skipping arm in arm with Peg ahead of Smiles and Elbert, laughed with her sister as if only they four tapped out carefree happiness on the wooden planks of the Boardwalk.

Elbert guided them to the stall with the record-making machine. A barker leaned from the counter enticing customers. "Fifty cents! Just four bits! And you can send your mama, your best gal, or even your best gal's best friend a recording of your very own voice. Yessiree, your very own voice on a record just like this'un here in my hand."

He held up a black disc the size of a dessert plate. "Right here. Right now. Step right up and send the homefolks a song, a message, a plea for bail. Fifty cents!"

June turned an expectant grin to Smiles. He fished a dollar from his billfold and handed it to her. "You, too," she crowed. "Right aftah me!"

The barker ushered June into what must surely have been a telephone booth at one time. He directed her to speak into a microphone and held up one finger. She nodded and as soon as he exited the booth, she began to sing a cappella Johnny Mercer's *Blues in the Night*. A loudspeaker attached to the stall's roof broadcast over the Boardwalk her slightly off-key recital.

"My mama done tol' me . . ." she warbled.

Passersby stopped to watch and listen, more than a few digging into their purses and pockets for a half dollar. What captivated them wasn't June's performance, but the girl herself. She was singing with her eyes closed, head back, swaying her head and hips. She was completely without reserve or self-consciousness. To see her was to want to be like her, to believe you could actually pull it off. She made it look so easy. So sensual.

As the barker promised, June emerged from the booth holding a black vinyl disc. Blank when he'd inserted it in the machine, it was now lined with grooves surrounding a pencil sized hole in ever extending circles. The barker took the newly minted record from June, holding it delicately with the palms of his hands. He smoothed a glued label bordering the center hole then placed the record in a paper sleeve.

"There ya go, cutie pie." He eyed the crowd at the counter and told June, "Come again soon now, hear? Who's next?"

June pushed Smiles forward. "I already paid for him, remembah?"

Inside the booth, having been warned by the barker with a somewhat threatening index finger for emphasis that there would be only one take and it began as soon as he closed the door, Smiles leaned into the microphone. Agonizingly aware of his Norfolk audience, the many people at home who would hear this recording, but forgetting that would include Grace, and the bullhorn over his head, he began to speak with the bluster that'd gotten him through many a tight squeeze.

"Hi, ever'body! How 'bout this? I'm talking my letter to you. Man, I'm telling you! Well, it's bee-U-tee-ful here in Virginia Beach. Everything's just as pretty as a tropical paradise. When I have leave I spend most my time over at the Herts' in Norfolk, though. They treat me real good. I couldn't ask for better friends. And man, can Pearl cook! Mom, she can make pies almost as good as you. If I don't watch out, I'll be a heavyweight. Hey, today I was in the ring with a professional who'd fought Tony Zale and Sugar Ray Robinson. How 'bout that? A real contender. Uncle Marne was there. He comes to all my fights when he's in port. Well, I guess I've told you that already. Hey, here's something. The Herts let me drive their Lincoln down here to the Boardwalk tonight. Man, is that livin'!"

111

Still leaning into the microphone, Smiles saw June winking at him as she leaned into the glass, inches from his face. He couldn't help himself. With a teasing Cheshire smile he crowed, "Neckin' in the back seat. Man, I'm tellin' ya!"

Smiles noted the timer attached to the recorder. "Well, I gotta go. Mom and Mother, I miss you. Dad and Pop, I'll be seein' ya. Sis and Presh, you be good but have fun! Don't forget not to take any wooden . . ."

A buzzer sounded. The recording was finished. Smiles exited the booth with his vinyl disc. The man took it from him in the same careful palms-against-edge manner he'd used with June but didn't ask him to come again; soon or any other time.

Holding June's hand as they leisurely strolled the Boardwalk back to her father's car, the ocean's waves rhythmically pounding the beach under a black sky dotted with countless brilliant stars, Smiles sighed happily. June moved her hand to his bicep and squeezed. She leaned her head into his muscled arm. Smiles' chest expanded as he sighed again, patting her silky cheek with a hand the size of a bear's claw, still redolent with the liberal dose of Old Spice he'd sprinkled into it following his shower and shave. June closed her eyes and smiled contentment as they walked.

Chapter Eighteen

December 1943

Her Story

"It's from Eddie!" Marlene shouted as she pulled a government-issued envelope from the mailbox. She let the lid of the black metal box clang shut, pulled open the screen door and allowed it to bang behind her as she hurried to her mother's overstuffed chair by the front window. Marlene had refused to take her turn to support the family following high school graduation. Instead, she'd gone with high school girlfriends to find work in exciting New York City, and was now home for the holidays.

"I don't know why I lost out on the Springwood job, Camille," she'd told her older sister with spite, "but you're going to pay for it with another year at home until Theta graduates. Hope it was worth it."

Though still so miffed with Marlene that she refused to speak to her, Camille, upon hearing the commotion, rushed down the stairs from the bedroom she'd been holed up in since her sister's holiday return. Theta hurried to the living room from the kitchen, dish towel in hand.

It was the afternoon mail, so all three were home, Camille from her monotonous job of assembling gears and pulleys for monstrous combines, and Theta from Richmond High School. It had seemed weeks and weeks since they'd heard from Eddie, who'd joined the Army just after Pearl Harbor. He'd hoped to become a pilot with the Army Air Corp, but instead was assigned to a baseball Service Team. President Roosevelt had said he thought baseball should continue not only to entertain troops but to also boost wartime morale. So, Eddie was stationed at the new

113

Santa Ana Air Base in California, keeping up morale.

"Hurry!" Camille said, impatient for her mother to tear off the end of the tissue-thin envelope. May Nelle tossed the ragged piece into her lap and blew into the packet to more easily extract the fragile stationery. Placing Peter's discarded reading glasses on her nose, she raised the letter to eye level.

"Dear Mom, C, M and Tooey . . . ," she began as Camille and Marlene rolled their eyes at the sound of their favored brother's pet name for Theta. *"You'd be surprised how hot it is here in southern California, even in winter. The Army has the team in Quonset huts on the base and it sure does get steamy. All day we're on the field practicing or playing exhibitions. Guess who's on my team? Joe DiMaggio! He's the only major league player here, but who else would we want??? We beat an Army team out of Texas yesterday. Semi-pros come from everywhere to play, too. Most of them are conscientious objectors or 4-F, and those guys are mostly over the hill, some as old as 40. But still good ball players. We been told we'll get to play the Navy team pretty soon. Bring 'em on!*

"Trey, he's our third baseman believe it or not, set me up with his wife's best friend a while back. She sure is pretty. Blonde hair, dimples. Almost looks like Donna Reed. And she's what they call out here perky. She's not like anybody I've ever met before. Swims in the ocean, cooks up a storm, works at the factory making shells. She can do anything."

Camille began to laugh. "Well, I guess there's gonna be *two* weddings in the family."

"Don't be silly," May Nelle objected crossly. "Eddie's not going to throw away his career just like that. Why, Ball State's holding his scholarship and after college the Redlegs may just decide he's worth a try. My word but you're silly!"

Theta studied her hands, suppressing a knowing smile. Eddie

had written her a week ago that he'd married that perky blonde from California. She wrote back that he should begin mentioning his wife in letters before springing the surprise. This, then, was his idea of a mention. It was hard for her to not laugh outright.

May Nelle continued reading. *"Hey, speaking of Donna Reed, I saw her at the USO in Los Angeles. Even prettier in real life. But what a surprise – she cusses like a sailor. Kinda made me look at her a little different. There were other movie stars there, too. They come to serve coffee and donuts and such.*

I'll be sending something to you for Christmas. Sorry it's going to be late. So watch for it and in the meantime take care of yourselves and stay warm. I guess if you keep the furnace as low as you used to, you'll have to think of me out here in all this heat. Yours, Eddie.

"P.S. Her name's Nanette but everybody calls her Cracker on account of she was a real firecracker even when she was little."

May Nelle harrumphed, folded the letter, and replaced it in the envelope. She tapped the letter against her knee and looked sternly at Camille. "I don't want to hear any more nonsense out of you. Now finish getting dressed. Theta's going to have supper on the table as soon as Peter gets home. Cracker my foot. What a name."

Camille risked another scowl. "We don't have to wait, do we? He's probably going to eat with Phyllis again. Mom, that's what happens when people get engaged. Haven't you noticed he doesn't hardly ever eat his suppers with us anymore?"

"Engaged at his age!" May Nelle waved Eddie's letter in the air, dismissing the pesky idea of Peter's impending marriage as well as that of her youngest son. "He's stayed at home this long, I don't know what in the world's got into him. Mercy!"

Theta was surprised by her mother's obstinate refusal to

acknowledge the obvious. Surely, she knew that Peter only dutifully stayed with the younger family until she graduated high school. She was the last, the one everybody was waiting to grow up and start not only bringing in a paycheck but also managing the house. Her mother couldn't be that far down the path of denial that she couldn't see what was so clear to everyone else.

"Should we wait, Mom?" Theta asked, in a tone that agreed with Camille.

"We'll wait."

Theta turned down the gas under the pot bubbling with great northern beans then went to the bedroom she shared with her mother. There she slipped out of her third-hand gray skirt, floral print blouse and slip. After pulling on a worn chenille robe, she took her clothes to the cellar where former tenants had left a wringer washer. Beside the enamel tub on a wooden drying rack hung the twice-handed-down plaid skirt and white blouse she'd washed the night before.

She filled the tub with just enough water and Rinso powder to make suds, then swished first the faded blouse then the gray skirt, and finally the yellowed slip in the freezing water. She emptied the tub, pushing the sudsy water into the drain with numb fingers. Theta then pressed down the cracked, rubber stopper and drew in another small amount of water from the lone tap. This was the part she hated, trying to get all the soap out of her clothes so they wouldn't be stiff the next day, yet also trying as best she could to protect her already stinging hands from the frigid water.

At last satisfied that the clothes were thoroughly rinsed, she tightly twisted the garments rather than putting them through the finger-hungry wringer. She hung each dripping piece on the wooden rack. She snatched the dried, wrinkled ones and hurried upstairs, wondering if this set of clothes resembled crepe from drying or if the life was nearly worn from every one of them.

"Still waiting, Mom?" she called unnecessarily as she brought the ironing board down like a Murphy bed built into the kitchen wall.

"He'll be along," came the resolute reply.

As the electric iron heated, Theta filled an empty Coca-Cola bottle with water. Using her thumb as a stopper, she doused the stiff skirt and blouse with uneven sprinkles then rolled them to retain moisture while they awaited pressing. She hummed as she ironed, satisfied with her precise work if not with the task.

Wear one clean outfit to school while the other dries. Repeat ad nauseam day after weary day.

"It's been a long time since Camille or Marlene have passed down anything," she mused quietly to herself as she pressed the iron into a blouse sleeve to make a precise crease shoulder to cuff. "I don't care. I like both these blouses better than any one of Camille's new ones anyway."

Theta hung the freshly ironed blouse on a wire hanger then carefully arranged the skirt on the ironing board. Guiding the iron rhythmically she sang, "Oh, I don't care, I don't care. This skirt is better anyway. Anyway. I like it better anyway. Anyway."

On impulse, she stuck out her tongue in the direction of her sisters' upstairs bedroom. With haughtily downturned mouth, she used safety pins to attach the smooth skirt to the blouse's hanger and turned the heat down for lightly pressing the wrinkles out of the slip that no one would see.

Lifting the ironing board to secure it back into its Murphy cubby, Theta called into the front room, "The beans are getting mushy, Mom."

"We wait."

Theta quietly removed a bowl from the cupboard and dished

up a healthy helping of the pallid beans flavored with chunks of fatty ham, careful to strain the meat from the broth so there would be some for Peter. Using the freshly ironed clothes to shield the bowl and spoon in her other hand, she crossed the living room where her mother still held vigil and slipped into their bedroom. She hung tomorrow's outfit from a hook then closed the door, calling again to the woman keeping watch by the front room window, "I guess I'll study until Peter gets home."

After she finished her supper, Theta shoved the bowl beneath the bed, planning to retrieve and wash it in the morning before her mother awakened. Propped on pillows on the sagging mattress, her stomach full, she opened *The Last of the Mohicans* hoping to finish her assignment though her eyes were already drooping. Shortly she was dreaming of the Long Carabine stalking in to rescue her from an icy dungeon where drab skirts hung over barred windows. The room was ominously dark when she was awakened by her mother beckoning from the front room.

May Nelle's call was demanding rather than plaintive. Junior had once likened it to his father calling a hog, the way her voice, when summoning Theta, began short and high-pitched then rose to a lingering squeal. "Theee-tahhhhhh!"

At first, she thought it was predawn and Georgeanne had arrived with the twins. Theta imagined her sister-in-law lowering the babies into the secondhand playpen. Georgeanne had happily returned to the Bucyrus Erie when the war took away most of the men. Though she'd lost her secretarial position, the assembly line was better than housework. It was Theta's job to feed her nephews and make sure their diapers were fresh before she left to catch the city bus to the high school. Heaven only knew what the boys did all day as their mamaw sat staring out the window, on watch for any neighborhood shenanigans.

"Okay. I'm coming," Theta answered sleepily. She glanced at the alarm clock as she pushed the book off her lap and swung her legs over the edge of the bed. "Midnight!"

Rushing into the front room, afraid her mother was having a spell, she found instead her Uncle Gilbert. He was swaying drunkenly, rubbing his hands together for both warmth and supplication. "It's too cold out there, May. I'll freeze to death, even on a hot-air grate. I won't be no trouble, and quiet as a little mouse. You can count on that."

"Theta," May Nelle said with resignation, "take Gilbert to his room."

"Has Peter come home?" Theta asked, ignoring her uncle's beseeching eyes.

"Not yet. But we may not have much time 'fore he does. Now take Gilbert to his room."

Turning her attention to her brother, who was wiping tears of relief from cheeks reddened by both the cold and masses of broken capillaries, May Nelle was stern. "Now, you must be quiet in there, Gilbert. If Peter finds you, there'll be a scene and you'll be put out even if it's colder than a witch's tit. And he just might toss us out with you."

"Oh, I swear I'll be quiet as a mouse, May. You won't hear no peep outta me."

Theta took her uncle's arm to help him to the kitchen to avoid his stumbling into an end table and breaking a lamp as he'd done the last time. "How Aunt Nola, with all her savvy, could marry this man is beyond anything I can imagine," she grumbled under her breath.

"And Mom having the nerve to say it was Aunt Nola's leaving him that drove him to drink. Like I'd be so naïve to

119

believe that. No one who didn't want to could be driven to waste their life in a bottle and end up without so much as two sticks to rub together."

No, she'd thought but not voiced to her mother on any of the occasions May Nelle had blamed Nola for her brother's sorry condition. Uncle Gilbert just wasn't the man they'd all thought back when he was young, extraordinarily handsome, and happily carefree. Back when he glibly married his first cousin just because she asked him to join her in revenge against her father, Gilbert's paternal uncle. At least she hadn't had to change her name, Nola had laughed. She'd envisioned a merry marriage with her jovial cousin, always the life of every party. Too late, but not long after the hasty Justice of the Peace wedding, did she realize that his was a flimsy façade.

"Come on, Uncle Gilbert, hurry up before Peter gets home."

They were passing through the kitchen. Still teetering, Gilbert leaned toward the bean pot on the range. "I hain't had a bite to eat, Theta. How's about you getting me some of them beans and bringin' 'em to my room?"

"Okay, but you have to be quiet," Theta said, guiding him toward the pantry. "Now you get in your room and I'll bring you some beans just as soon as I get your bedding."

Obediently, May Nelle's brother stumbled into the larder. It was the one place Peter would never step foot. Theta reached up to yank the string hanging from the lone bulb then closed the door.

"Mom," she said as she passed through the living room, "I know you weren't serious, but Peter really is going to throw all of us out if he ever finds out you've been hiding Uncle Gilbert."

May Nelle lifted a weary face. "Doesn't matter. Camille's our breadwinner now. I guess ever'body's right. Peter's done left us. Marlene's left and Camille will, too. But you won't.

You'll stay with Mommy. When you graduate you'll get a good job. We'll be fine. You and me; we'll be just fine."

May Nelle plopped her head back onto the hand-tatted damask that covered the back of her chair. "Ohhh," she wailed. "I tried and tried to keep us all together. And now Peter's done left us already anyhow, along with the others."

Theta ignored with contempt the tears dropping onto her mother's cheeks. What she really wanted to do was shake May Nelle. Didn't she realize that Peter had sacrificed years and years of his own happiness to loyally support her and his four younger siblings? And just when Eddie would have gone into the workforce, there was the war. Peter, with wooden resignation, had trudged further into servitude.

Sighing beneath her breath, Theta continued to the bedroom for the pallet they kept in the closet for these subzero nights when Uncle Gilbert was sure to show up. "Peter's left us," she muttered spitefully as she stooped to reach into the back of the closet she shared with her mother, putting emphasis on the finality of his long suffering.

"But not me," she grumbled sarcastically. "Oh, no. Never me." Sounding much like her mother, not in heartbreak but in frustration, she moaned hopelessness.

After settling Gilbert on his pallet of old quilts on the pantry floor, Theta got his supper. Dipping into the pot, she saw that it was down by more than a bowl or two. And much of the scant meat gone, too. For the second time that night, she raised two resentful eyes and one stabbing tongue to her sisters' room above the peeling kitchen ceiling.

"Now eat this up, Uncle Gilbert. This light has to go out before Peter gets home. If he sees it, he might open the door to shut it off. He's a stickler for lights left burning."

Shoving a spoonful of meatless beans into his mouth, Gilbert nodded. Theta closed the door and began ridding up the table where Camille and Marlene had obviously had their suppers then left their dishes. There were only two bowls and spoons. May Nelle had stubbornly waited to eat.

Theta didn't hold irrational optimism that Peter would have a late supper with the woman obstinately waiting in the living room. She ladled overcooked beans into a soup bowl and set it aside for her mother then poured what was left into a crock. She filled the sink with hot water, swished in an economic dollop of Palmolive then went to the pantry where Uncle Gilbert was snoring loudly, the empty bowl tilted crazily on his chest. She took up the dish, and before turning off the bulb took another disapproving look at the wasted life sprawled on the narrow floor.

She did up the dishes and was just hanging the dish towel on the hook by the sink when she saw the headlights of Peter's 1931 Pontiac coupe move hauntingly across the kitchen wall. Quickly she turned on the radio and busied herself by setting the table for the twins' breakfast. Peter came through the door just as she was setting a box of Cream of Wheat on the counter next to the range. He glanced at the radio.

"What you got that thing on so late for? Turn it off. You're burning electricity."

"I will, Peter. I'm just finishing up here in the kitchen. We waited for you."

As she knew he would, upon hearing the last he turned a guilty back to her. He shuffled out of the kitchen slinging his own frustration as he went. "It don't need to be turned up so loud anyway. We got neighbors. Now hurry up. And don't forget to turn off the light."

Theta waited until she heard his footsteps on the stairs before turning off the radio. She took up the bowl of beans for her mother and headed to the living room. "Mom, did you hear Peter come in? Here's some supper for you. He already had his."

May Nelle took the bowl and raised the spoon to her lips. She chewed and swallowed. "Theta, these beans is ruined. You've let 'em overcook."

Chapter Nineteen

December 1943

His Story

The Old Man, who was in actuality in his mid-forties, briskly rubbed Smiles' shoulder muscles. It had been an easy fight, but Smiles seemed tense as he laid on the training table following his match that ended in another knock out. "Loosen up, kid. These here shoulders are like knots. You're gonna have spasms if ya don't relax."

"That's not what I'm afraid of," Smiles said to his trainer. "Did you see that guy?"

"Yeah, I seen 'im. Seen 'im go down lickity split." the Old Man laughed through phlegm unendingly rumbling in his throat.

"No, I'm talkin' about his eyes. Did ya see his eyes? He was wanting me to hit him. The guy was punch drunk."

"So what? The fight was legit. You did 'im a favor gettin' it over so fast."

Smiles leaned on an elbow, swung his legs over the side of the massage table and hopped off. "No, he did me one. I'm not fighting anymore."

The Old Man stopped screwing the cap onto the opaque glass bottle. "You ain't serious. They put guys in the brig for that, ya know."

Smiles tossed the wet towel to the Old Man, as he shrugged into his grandmother's satin robe with the Golden Gloves title confidently embroidered above the left breast. "I'm not leaving the Navy. I'm just leaving the ring."

He headed to the showers, already planning what he'd say to the Naval Boxing Team commander first thing in the morning. But now he needed to suds up. June was waiting supper again.

His mind wasn't on how she might react to his decision, but what might be on her table. Now that his resolution had released him from the dread of a future that mirrored tonight's punch-drunk pugilist, he suddenly realized he was famished.

Smiles loved the meals Pearl Hert set on her lace covered table. Somehow the tomatoes seemed juicier and the corn sweeter. She and Preston put these familiar garden vegetables alongside smooth dishes of grits and black-eyed peas, foods neither his mother nor Mom ever dished up. And their cornbread was dense with crust crisply fried in an iron skillet, not like cornbread as sweet and light as cake that Mom baked in deep pans in her oven. While he'd give anything to taste Mom's cooking, or his mother's, it was the Herts' Southern fare that he'd come to crave, washed down with sweet tea instead of bitter black coffee.

He could hear laughter as he hurried up the Herts' walk. All the doors and windows were open to let in the fresh salty air of Norfolk's winter night. He stepped onto the porch and was just raising his fist to knock on the wooden screen door when he was stopped by a giggle coming from the night.

"Y'all ready to sit down ta suppah?"

Turning to his right, Smiles made out the white of June's blouse. She was sitting on the porch swing hidden from the sidewalk by a trellis of clematis. The disembodied blouse rose and fell with the motion of the swing. He followed it with his eyes. "You bet. But not before . . ."

"I get a kiss," she finished, rising.

Smiles caught her as she bounced like a gymnast to encircle his waist with slender, long legs. Hugging his neck, she planted a firm kiss on his lips. Setting her down, he could see that her blouse was tied in a knot at her waist, allowing a generous peep of tanned midsection. Though the night was becoming chilly she wore loose linen trousers. She was barefoot, too, he noted with affection.

"Let's not go in just yet," he said, pulling her toward the porch swing.

She threw back her head and laughed. "That's lateh, sugah. Mama's waitin' suppah."

Reluctantly, Smiles allowed himself to be led inside where candles burned on the dining room table. Preston was already seated, knife and fork at attention in his ready hands. June laced her fingers in Smiles' and raised on tiptoes to bus his cheek before seating him beside her father.

"Well?" asked Preston.

"Out like a light, first round," Smiles said, sounding more pleased than he felt.

"Atta boy!" Preston leaned back, tipping his chair to call into the kitchen, "We've got a hungry sailor out here, girls. Snap it up!"

Through a swinging door Pearl led her daughters carrying trays of food that smelled so good Smiles' stomach embarrassingly growled. He didn't need a light to know the belles were bearing a Dutch oven of ham hocks and snapped green beans that Pearl had put up last summer. Ordinarily it'd be served with new potatoes, platters of bulbous green onions and freshly sliced beefsteak tomatoes, and a dish of thick cucumber wheels swimming with rings of Vidalia onions in iced vinegar and olive oil heavily seasoned with salt and pepper.

But it didn't matter on this cool winter night that there were no fresh vegetables; Peg was carrying a platter of crisp cornbread. He breathed deeply and exhaled a sigh so filled with satisfaction that the four Herts bawled laughter.

Preston delivered a blessing so brief that Smiles wondered if he should continue grace behind his own closed eyes. "Here, boy, you start the cornbread around while I dish up the beans," June's father urged.

Smiles took a square of cornbread and passed the plate to June. He took a generous slab of Pearl's fresh churned sweet butter from a delicate Limoges saucer, spread it thickly on the thin cornbread and took a bite. In the candlelight he saw he had chewed half a mealworm baked into the hunk still in his hand. Beyond the yellow square with the telltale partial worm, he could see Pearl awash in the radiance of candlelight happily accepting a plate of green beans from her husband.

"What's wrong, honey?" June asked. "Will you pass on the buttuh?"

Smiles swallowed and quickly stuffed the rest of the polluted cornbread into his mouth. "This is so good, I forgot my manners. Here you go; let me hold the dish for you."

As promised, after helping to clear the table and pulling on a sweater, June led Smiles to the porch swing. They sat close together, June's legs tucked beneath her as she leaned into Smiles' shoulder. His arm rested on the back of the swing just above her neck. He propped his chin on her hair and breathed in a lingering scent of flowers. Something familiar, he wasn't sure whether it was lilac or rose. The swing gently swayed forward and back as he pushed with the balls of his feet against the wooden planks of the porch. Crickets and frogs trilled their songs of romance. From inside came muted laughter; the others were gathered around the Galvin listening to Jack Benny.

"Daddy's fixin' to come to your next fight," June mused lazily.

Smiles set his feet flat on the floor and the swing abruptly stopped. June sat up and looked at Smiles with suspicious eyes. "What's the mattuh?"

"I've been wondering how to bring it up and I guess now's

the time," Smiles said.

June cried when he finished. "You know what this means? You'll be shipped out."

Smiles nodded, pulling her close again. "Yes, I know. But I'd rather face that than see that guy's punch-drunk face in my mirror. Don'tcha get it? He wanted to be hit, was hoping for it. He was a goner. I don't want to ever get like that. And I didn't like polishing him off, bein' a party to his sickness. I didn't win, June; he lost."

"But you won't get like him, honey. You haven't lost a fight. Besides, what'll I do with y'all gone?"

"Write me. Stay true."

"Shoot. That's easier said than done. Look at Peg. Ever since Elbert shipped out, she doesn't go anywhere, doesn't do anything. She's miserable, and it's only been a coupla weeks. I don't know if I could stand it. 'Sides, Christmas isn't long off. Don't leave me with Christmas around the corner."

"It's not just bein' afraid of getting punch-drunk, June. It's the war. Look. Just like you said; Elbert's already shipped out. Most everybody is. All my friends from back home are. Don't you think it's time I go, too?"

June crossed her arms and pouted with her lower lip like a spoiled child. Her eyebrows came together in deep creases and she huffed her silent response.

"It's time, June."

"For me," June begged coyly, uncrossing her arms to run a finger along Smiles' jaw. She was adept at getting her way. "Just for a little bit more. Please, with sugah on it?"

She pinched his chin and brought his face to hers. Kissing his cheek, then drawing his earlobe into her mouth, she sighed a tune. "I don't want to be without you just yet. Please, sugah? Jus' til after my birthday?"

Accepting nibbles from his ear to his cheek and leading to his mouth, Smiles closed his eyes and tried to think when her birthday was. Of course: June. He began to protest when she covered his mouth with first gentle fingertips then her lips.

"Just til after my birthday," she whispered, drawing back to search his face with pitifully glistening eyes.

Smiles held her head in his hand just above the nape of her silky neck and wrapped his other arm around her waist to draw her in. He leaned her backward, supporting her so she wouldn't tense for fear of falling. He kissed the soft flesh below her jaw. Tilting her chin, he kissed her cheek along the peach fuzz near her ear. As his lips reached hers, June brought both hands to the sides of his head to make his kisses hers.

And that's what he liked, a woman in control.

Chapter Twenty

Spring 1944

Her Story

May Nelle was not happy. First, she was forced to lumber all the way downtown to the Hoosier Store to buy the blasted things, and now these newfangled underdrawers were causing her all kinds of embarrassment. She'd outgrown her panties and finally had to admit she needed a larger pair.

She blamed the war for her current predicament. It was bad enough that there were all kinds of inconveniences on the home front, like the rationing of sugar for her pies and the return of unsliced bread. Now she'd have to wear unmentionables secured at the waist with buttons. At the moment, these britches were anything but secure.

"Why in the sorry world can't they just leave us enough rubber for elastic?" she complained to Theta, who was trying to shield her face from recognition by anyone passing by on Main Street.

She and her mother were huddled against the recessed corner of the display window outside Dumond's Notions. May Nelle was looking fervently up and down the sidewalk, the new panties a pool at her feet. "Hurry up, Theta, pull 'em up!"

"Mom, you're going to have to step out of them. I can't pull them up right here in the middle of Main Street," Theta hissed.

She'd known, but hadn't dared to suggest at the sales counter, that her mother needed to buy another size larger. May Nelle had insisted on wearing the tight new panties out of the store, her tattered ones saved to take home in the Bartel's

Hoosier Store paper bag in the expectation they could be worn again once she lost these few pounds.

Even though Theta had her reservations about the size of the new underwear, she never dreamed that the button would give way, and pop with such force that even she heard it bounce against her mother's long black skirt just moments before the panties slid to the sidewalk.

"I am not going to be seen in public without my necessaries!" May Nelle said.

Theta bit her lip. She'd had to ditch her last class, the first time she'd ever done such a thing, to help her mother get to town to buy the underwear before school let out. "Why can't I just buy them for you after school?" she pointlessly asked that morning. And now here she was, her classmates already passing by on foot; in city buses; and most horrifying to Theta, in their daddy's cars.

Turning her face close to her mother's, hoping no one would recognize her faded gray skirt and worn print blouse, she pleaded, "Just step out, Mom. If I pull up these pants, your legs and you-know-what are going to show.

"And anyway, then how will you keep them up after that?"

May Nelle grumbled but lifted first one foot then the other as Theta pulled the now buttonless panties from around her mother's feet and quickly stashed them in the paper sack holding the older but more securely tight underwear.

She looked up in humiliated frustration as she stood, her eyes focused just beyond her mother's reddening face. May Nelle was staring daggers at curious passersby, her jaw thrust out in furious indignation. Behind her mother Theta could see a brilliant Singer Sewing Machine displayed in the window. At its wrought iron feet were various colored buttons tossed like confetti. On an easel beside the machine was propped a magazine ad that was glued to cardboard.

It declared in large script, "Please, Singer: I have a problem!"

Despite her best efforts to hold it in, Theta burst into laughter. May Nelle turned her ire on her daughter, prompting more laughter through hands pressed against nose and mouth so tight Theta couldn't wipe away the tears streaming uncontrolled down the sides of her face.

"Wait til I get you home, young lady," May Nelle bellowed as she stepped from the shelter of the recessed window with its mocking display. Theta followed her, stumbling down the street, nearly doubled over as she tried to control her amusement. Window shoppers turned to stare at the angry bustle that was her mother, unaware of the indignity beneath the furiously flouncing black sateen skirt. Their wondering faces only fed Theta's sense of the ridiculous.

May Nelle strode ramrod straight toward home, her nose lifted into the atmosphere above her defiant chin. Theta's laughter descended into chuckles then erupted anew as she recalled her mother's furious expression against the backdrop of the impertinent display. She followed at a distance until they neared the latest of their downward spiraling rentals. Close to home, she called an ignored adieu to her mother as she turned into an unpaved alley.

Opening the door to a two-story frame garage, she coughed away the last of her laughter. "Sorry I'm late, Mr. Howell. I had to take Mom to town. I'll stay til all my work's done."

Clarence Howell looked up from his desk. "I was beginning to worry about you, Theta. It's not like you to be late. I was just about to call and check on you when I remembered you haven't got a telephone. It really is a necessity, you know."

Pulling a large white apron over her head and knotting it

tight at her waist to protect her blouse and skirt, Theta nodded futile agreement and hurried to a wobbly three-legged stool. She sat long hours on the unforgiving oak seat, tediously filling jar after jar with grape jelly hot from the spout. Or maybe today it would be strawberry. She looked at the empty syrup containers discarded in the corner to determine which flavor would be spurting from the valves of the huge copper cooker Mr. Howell had installed in his garage. Grape.

To her right, on a long workbench, were wooden Coca-Cola cases filled with sterilized glass jars. It was her job to fill the twelve-ounce hobstar jars then screw on lids as tight as her small hands could manage. On a similar workbench to her left were stacked empty Coca-Cola cases. She would soon pack those with dozens of jars of cooling jelly.

Once in a while she imagined her mother's screech inside the ad. "Please, Singer: I have a problem!" and unconsciously chuckled aloud.

Slow hours later, when the thick jelly from the cooker became lazy dollops, Theta carried the cases of filled jars to a former tool bench against the back wall where the Howells' teenage neighbor, Donnie Homer, would seal the lids. Her back ached, but she unwittingly beamed. A rare expression any time, but especially near midnight with another day of school scant hours ahead. The looping memory of her mother's irritation and apt advertisement had kept her amused all evening.

"Don't see your smile all that much," Donnie said in the shy way he had with girls. "It's nice."

Theta was gluing a label to a jar identifying it as Howell's Homemade Concord Jelly. Donnie stood hunch-shouldered beside her, passing finished jars to her for the application of the labels. A quiet boy whose fatherless family struggled nearly as much as her own, he rarely spoke to anyone here or at school.

Though he towered above his peers, he seemed with his hunched shoulders to be insignificantly small.

"What were you laughing about?" he continued quietly, brushing her fingers as he handed her a jar.

Theta shrugged, suddenly embarrassed.

"Come on," he uncharacteristically urged. "I got up at six to deliver papers, and I've been here ever since school got out. I got studies to do before I can get to bed. So, don't ya think I deserve a laugh? Tell me what's so funny."

Just thinking about the incident and the impossibility of describing it to her male classmate caused Theta to titter. She nearly dropped a jar of jelly as she lifted a hand to hide her open mouth with its set of crooked teeth. She shook her head and attempted without success to control her laughter.

"I can't," she finally managed.

The two worked in silence as they usually did, Theta forcing herself to suppress the image of her mother's hilarious indignity by replacing it with images of movie tickets on a spool; she tearing one red rectangle after another to pass to other, less burdened classmates. From the image of the Tivoli Theater's ticket booth, her thoughts drifted to other unencumbered contemporaries shoving dimes at her for Springwood Lake popcorn.

Following graduation, she would return to the concession stand, adding it to her two winter jobs. Her own fault, she knew. If she hadn't caused the rift between her sisters, Marlene wouldn't have mulishly left for the Big Apple.

Marlene's traitorous abdication meant to Camille another year of contributing her meager salary to supplement Peter's men's wages. To poor Gilbert it meant another year of dodging his nephew's eagle eyes and ire. They now anxiously awaited Theta's high school graduation when she would at last become their liberator and her mother's source of consolation and sole support.

From the depths of imagining a three-job menial life sentence, not counting duties at home, Theta's amusement turned to heart sinking despair. Without much effort, she'd been successful in squelching this night's joy. Scowling, she began to silently chant her mantra of late: "I will go to Earlham. I will not work in a factory all my life. I will go to Earlham. I will not work in . . ."

"Anyway," Donnie said as he saw her mouth turn downward, "I liked it."

He handed her another finished jar. "Your smile. Looked pretty. You should do it more often."

Theta slowly slid a gluey label onto the cooling glass, being overly careful to make sure it was centered. She couldn't think of anything to say back to him, frowning at the thought that he was probably joking. She silently started the pledge again as her thumbs meticulously leveled the paper label.

"Say," he said slowly, "anybody ask you to prom yet?"

Theta shook her head, glancing sideways at him as she received another sealed jar.

"Wanna go with me?"

The glass jar with all its warm contents shattered on the packed dirt of the garage floor. Theta didn't know what surprised her most: that Donnie Homer was actually talking, or that he was actually asking her on a date. And to prom at that.

Two weeks later she pulled Camille's third-hand formal over her head to see if it would fit for the senior prom, her first dance, formal or otherwise. Theta was as nervous as she'd been the night she broke the jelly jar. Still, she admired the way Camille's dress perfectly draped over her shoulders to fall effortlessly over hips to barely dust the floor as if it'd been bought just for her.

She turned to the side to see the effect of the movement in the grainy mirror over her mother's dressing table.

Smoothing the rows and rows of peach taffeta that caused the formal's skirt to billow into a wide sphere around her feet, Theta grinned at her reflection. She remembered how Camille had worked extra hours at Woolworth's to buy the gown for her own senior prom, and how Marlene had been as radiant as Camille when she wore it the next year.

"And now it's my turn," Theta said to the girl in the mirror. She blinked, surprised. Was that really her? Could she be almost as lovely as Camille? Maybe as pretty as Marlene? "I don't look like Mom after all. I don't look like her!"

The dress, and Donnie's invitation, had transformed her. "All because I laughed."

The next day she made a point to smile at students as they passed in hallways between classes and was rewarded with smiles in return. Many were paired with curious eyes as if she were new to the school. In a way she was. What started as an experiment had become in the past couple weeks an altering determination.

"It's like I'm a whole different person," she said to her friend Sue after JoAnna Hill, one of the popular girls in the running for prom queen, had flashed a pretty smile in return as she'd passed in the school hallway. "But I haven't changed at all. I'm still me wearing the same two frumpy skirts day after day, yet somehow it's like they've never seen me before."

Sue turned her head to watch JoAnna with her carefree entourage gaily skip down the stairwell. "Do you really think she knows who you are?" she asked.

"That's not the point. The point is that she saw me. She looked at me and reacted. Sue, I've never had people look at me before!"

"I didn't think you wanted them to. All you ever want to do is sit at home."

Theta's eyebrows narrowed as she remembered her mother's disapproval upon hearing she'd accepted a date. "Oh, Sue, you know that's not true. You know Mom likes me to stay home with her. And, I guess before Donnie said what he did, I just didn't think there was much to look at. Camille and Marlene have always been the pretty ones. But somehow when Donnie asked me to prom, and said I looked pretty, well, I . . . I don't know. It was the very first time I didn't think I looked frumpy. The first time I realized that I don't look like . . ."

She shrugged, holding her books close to her bosom. "I can't explain it, Sue. All I know is that night walking home from work at the Howell's, I thought about what Donnie said and decided I'd try to smile more and see what happened."

"And?"

"And you see for yourself," Theta beamed. "People notice me. They are looking *at* me, not through me. And they're smiling back!"

Sue nodded, gazing absently over her friend's head. "Maybe I shoulda started smiling, too. Maybe I'd be going to prom."

Theta touched her arm. "It's not too late."

"It is," Sue nearly spat, looking harshly into Theta's hazel eyes. "And it's too late for you, too, really. If you'd started your little experiment earlier, maybe you'd have other friends. Maybe even be up for queen. Or at least not going to prom with Donnie Homely."

Theta sharply withdrew her hand from Sue's arm. "Why, Sue, what a mean thing to say."

Sue shrugged as she brushed past, leaving Theta open-mouthed but not smiling.

Chapter Twenty-one

Spring 1944

His Story

Smiles was defeated. At least it felt that way. He stood on one side of the referee, his opponent on the other. Both boxers heaved exhausted, battered breaths as they waited to hear the decision. Smiles had never been in this position and he didn't like it. He raised a gloved hand to wipe away sweat trailing toward his swelling eye. Like the other sailor, he shuffled his feet and bounced lightly; a sure sign of nerves overcoming fatigue.

A judge leaned through the ropes to hand the referee a folded note. The official resumed his place between the fighters before taking a look. He then held aloft the arm of Smiles' opponent. "The winner by a split decision . . ."

Thinking back on that December night on the porch swing with June, Smiles was filled with regret. He'd never lost a fight. Til now.

As his gloves were being unlaced in the dingy dressing room, Smiles told the Old Man, "Maybe I should've hung up the gloves like I wanted, after I fought that guy who was begging to be hit, he was so punch drunk."

"Kid, don't take it so hard. You know how many guys box as long as you without a defeat on their record? And a split decision ain't no real defeat. One judge scored ya the winner."

"Even if two judges scored me the winner, it wouldn't be a clean win."

"You think Brownie's in the showers thinking he didn't take the fight tonight? I frickin' guarantee ya he ain't."

"If so, only 'cause he got the decision and maybe doesn't

care it wasn't clear cut," Smiles said, unrolling the tape from around his left hand. "But I would."

The Old Man studied Smiles' face. "I'll tell ya who the loser is and it ain't on account of no fight. It's you and it's on account of your attitude. You ain't got a good attitude."

Smiles threw the length of soiled tape in a trash container and began unrolling the wrappings from his right hand. "You're wrong there. I do have a good attitude. Because I'm making a decision and it's unanimous. You know why? Because I'm gonna go write the commander right now requesting transfer to active duty in the Pacific, and I'm gonna put it in his box tonight before anybody can overrule me."

Two months later Smiles was ordered to active duty aboard the USS Randolph, an Essex-class aircraft carrier to be launched out of Newport News June 28, 1944. So, Smiles thought, happily reading his orders again, he was keeping his promise to June after all.

June had pouted for a while but was there to witness Rose Gillette swing the wrapped champagne bottle into the Randolph's long hull, sending the ship and her former pugilist boyfriend into the Atlantic. Smiles was amid the hundreds of sailors standing in mass formation on the flight deck as the ship slipped ceremoniously into the Newport News harbor. She thought she'd be able to make him out among the throng of swabs, but in the end couldn't see anything but a hazy blur of figures standing side by side as straight as a dark blue picket fence. She didn't know whether to continue waving her hanky or use it to wipe her weeping nose.

Smiles could see June almost as if a spotlight singled her out from the sea of waving hankies. She was the prettiest girl on the dock, her white hat a halo surrounding shining gossamer hair framing an angelic face. He watched her wave the handkerchief with the lavender crocheted edge his mother had sent her just that week. He saw her reluctantly drop her arm then bring the hanky to her nose. He could swear he saw her shoulders heave. And then she turned, disappearing into the crowd.

"Trinidad! We're goin' to Trinidad!" the sailor next to him enthused. "Man, I heard about them native girls. Yeah, baby!"

Smiles knew they were headed to Trinidad for their shakedown cruise but didn't know anything about the island or its natives. Still, he held out his hand and grinned as he introduced himself.

"Call ya Smiles, eh? Guess I can see why. Me, I'm Jim Watkins. You can call me Watkins, that's all right. Say, didja know we're gonna be plank owners?"

"Huh?"

"First men to serve on a new vessel. Every single one of us guys onboard today gets a title to a plank on this here flight deck. A real certificate to prove we was the original crew."

Smiles looked across the broad flat deck and then at the hundreds of men lining its perimeter. He stamped his foot. "I call this one right here. It's my June plank. After my girl."

"That one's yours, then," Jim said. "I guess I'll lay claim to that one over there. Gonna call her Hildie. You don't need to know why. Just gonna say it don't mean no tyin' the knot. Her old man owns a elevator comp'ny. Lord knows I don't need to get mixed up in no job that has ups and downs."

Smiles laughed at the deep wink with which Jim sealed both his claim and joke. With his GOB hat tilted rakishly over his right eye, Jim easily could have been the inspiration for Popeye's pappy.

"Hildie it is!" he agreed.

That night Smiles wrote his mother a letter enthusiastic with optimistic expectation.

"... *this is a big deal, I guess. A plank owner of this brand new, great big powerful aircraft carrier! Watkins says we're going to get a real title. I'll send it to you as soon as I get it.*

"*We sailed over to the Norfolk Naval Yard and the Herts got to come aboard this afternoon. I showed them 'my' plank. It was real special with all the officers standing on the bridge. I can't help being proud of her and being proud to be one of the first to serve aboard her. This ship is going to help put an end to this war. We're taking a short shakedown cruise -- you know, just to train all us greenhorns before we head to sea. Don't worry, though, because we probably won't see action. I've been told we'll be doing nothing but drilling all day long. That's ok with me. All the men aboard this ship are top notch. We're ready to get out to sea and like I say, put an end to this war.*

"*I don't want you to worry about me. Like I said, we probably won't be getting into any battles and there's good men on this ship. I got two new friends already. Besides Watkins I met a guy named Bob Kelly. We're all torpedomen.*

"*Well, I've got to get to mess. But I want you to know before I sign off that I'm reading my Bible every day. Give Mom a big kiss and tell Dad, Pop, Sis and Presh not to worry. When you write, please send pictures. I want to show Watkins and Kelly what a swell family I've got. Grace already sent one of her. I'm in it, too.*

"*All my love, Smiles.*"

The letter, as it turned out, was right about the shakedown cruise. It lasted less than three weeks. The urgency to get to the Pacific was palpable as the crew spent day after day drilling. By the time the Randolph pulled anchor from Trinidad, Smiles was sure he'd be seeing June for Christmas. Had even thought of asking his parents to come with Mom and Pop for Christmas in Norfolk. He was building the courage to tell them how serious he was about June, wondering if it was time to let them know their hopes for him and Grace probably wouldn't be realized, when Kelly came running into the torpedo room.

"We ain't goin' back to Norfolk! We're headed to the Panama Canal!"

Prevailing winds of urgency quickly changed course to disappointment. But the Randolph's sailors headed into it with fierce determination to overcome their holiday homesickness. They knew that shared enthusiasm to join the fight in the Pacific was essential to general morale.

"Panama Canal!" Smiles echoed, elbowing Watkins. "Hear that? We're gonna go through the Panama Canal!"

"Yeah, I'll buy tickets to that," Jim said with a crooked smile. "Be like a zebra through a needle."

Not quite, but like Jim's faulty analogy, it was close. Most men on deck could reach out and touch the walls of the famous locks as the thirty-six-ton carrier slowly sailed within what seemed to be inches of the passage linking the Atlantic with the Pacific. More than one sailor said as if he originated the idea, "One more coat of paint and the Randy couldn't a got through."

Drilling and more drilling filled the time aboard ship before it sailed into the San Francisco harbor just in time for a New Year's Eve leave. Kelly helped Watkins tie his scarf into a square sailor's knot. "Hold still. You act like you got ants in your pants."

"Hurry up, will ya?" Watkins urged. "The girls is waitin'! Hey, Smiles, change your mind. Come with us. We'll howl in 1945!"

"Can't do it. I volunteered for duty. Besides, we're getting mail call and man, am I ready. Hope Mom sent some cookies."

He wasn't disappointed. There were three packages of homemade cookies in his mail. Mom's were oatmeal raisin, as were his mother's. They knew what he liked and had timed the baking for the Randolph's expected arrival in San Francisco. Grace had sent an assortment of Christmas sugar cookies, intact but hard as nails.

And then there was the package from June.

"Look at this." Smiles laughed to himself, bent over her Sunshine Box, as she called it, on his lap, his legs swinging off the narrow side of his bunk. He took from the box two tins of cashews and pecans, several pieces of creamy divinity and soft logs of homemade caramels twisted into strips of waxed paper, date bars that could be mistaken for squares of cake safeguarded in tin foil so wrinkled that it must've been the last of the Herts' cache, and a Mason jar affixed with a paper label reading "Star Wishes" written in June's adolescent balloon cursive.

Inside the canning jar were dozens of colorful and oddly cut pieces of paper that resembled confetti. Munching on a date bar, he opened the vessel and pulled from it a green slip of construction paper the size of a cookie's fortune.

"Happy dreams of you-know-who," Smiles read before choosing a bright pink piece. "A soft pillow to lay your darling head."

Instructions written along the bottom of the glitter-bedecked label directed him to read one message every night before going to sleep. He was tempted to read them all, but dutifully screwed on the lid before placing June's Jiminy Cricket wishes under his pillow. He unwrapped a caramel, popped it into his mouth and turned his attention to a package from his Aunt Lillie, Opal's equally severe sister, though he knew her demeanor to be merely skin-deep.

She'd sent a small silk handkerchief as thin as paper. An

eagle was embroidered in one corner with "U.S. NAVY" sewn across it in red. Tucked inside was a note written in pencil.

"Smiles, I am going to give you this handkerchief that your dad sent me when he was away in the navy in WWI. I had always thought I would give it to you when you grew up. See if you can take good care of it as long as I have. It has been in my trunk all the while. Now don't let it get lost. It is worth taken care of. From Aunt Lillie."

Smiles tenderly folded the note inside the handkerchief and placed the small bundle in his wallet. He knew what she really meant when she asked him to take good care of it.

Finally, he opened a letter from his mother. He was disappointed that no pictures fell from the envelope but smiled as he read until he reached the last paragraph. The corners of his mouth fell briefly before he leaned his head back and laughed as he hadn't in months.

"It so pleases me and Mom," she'd written, *"to hear that you're reading your Bible every day. And if you would unzip it, you will find several photographs of all of us."*

Chapter Twenty-two

New Year's Eve 1944

Her Story

They were all disappointed when Eddie wrote just after Thanksgiving that he wouldn't be home for Christmas again this year. In fact, May Nelle felt she'd spoken for them all when she said it was the greatest disappointment of her life. But that was before she received the letter from Cracker.

May Nelle nearly fainted. It appeared that she had. With the letter open in her hand, she'd slumped in her chair by the front window. Her eyes rolled to her forehead until only the whites peeked below fluttering lids. Her mouth slacked to such an extreme that her chins unfurled to a creased, cushiony pillow. Theta, who'd been warily watching her mother as she silently read, jumped to her aid just as May Nelle lifted both hands to dramatically cover her eyes and groaned.

So, Theta thought, the cat's out of the bag. She took the letter from her mother's lap where it'd been dropped like so much trash. The stationery matched the perfumed envelope that Theta had brought in from the afternoon mail. When she'd seen the return address carefully printed on the extravagant blue vellum, she placed her thumb over "Mrs. E.A. Whittle" as she handed the envelope to her mother.

"Why, Mom!" Theta gasped after reading the letter. "She might be waiting for us at the depot this very minute!"

Theta's eyes swept the room. It was clean as a whistle, of course, but now she swiftly noted that threadbare armrests couldn't be hidden under damasks. Scratches in woodwork might be camouflaged by rubbings with dark crayons, but with a sinking stomach she could see there was simply too much to do to sufficiently mask the dilapidated furniture inside this worn-down house.

"Darn the post office!" she said, ignoring May Nelle's moans.

"How could he? How could he?" her mother pitifully repeated.

"This letter was mailed over a week ago. What's taken it so long to get here? Well, there's nothing left to do but for one of us go to the depot while the other tries to make this place as presentable as we can," Theta said, closing her eyes to the pathetic circumstances of their meager existence. If she didn't see it, she irrationally thought, it wouldn't be there.

Behind her lids she saw herself welcoming Cracker into a happy home however humble. So happy, that her sister-in-law would see only fresh flowers and crystal rainbows even if there weren't any.

"How could he? My boy! He was going to play ball after college, probably with the Redlegs! We was all going to Cincinnati!"

"Mom, stop it," Theta said irritably. "He's still your boy. He's still going to play ball." She didn't mention her mother's dream of moving to Cincinnati, just upriver from Louisville. "Let's not think about that now. Let's get ready for his wife—"

"His wife! How could he! How could he! Ohh!"

Theta read Cracker's letter again, written in royal blue ink with sweeping forward-leaning script. "She says she's so looking forward to meeting us, to being a part of our family, and expects to be here before the New Year, depending on train delays. Mom, it's New Year's Eve now. My gosh, she could pull up to the curb in a taxi at any minute."

"A taxi! What could she be thinking, spending that kind of money? What has Eddie gone and done? Married a gold-digger, that's what!"

"He's married someone he loves, Mom. And somebody who loves him."

May Nelle didn't respond to Theta's dreamy rationale. She was staring out the window now, anger reinforcing her reconnaissance. "Well, if she thinks we're going to pay the cab fare she's got another think coming!"

"I didn't mean she was going to pull up in a taxi right now. I meant that if we don't get to the depot, she might have to resort to that."

"Don't talk to me in that tone, Theta Marie. I have had a terrible blow. Your brother has married without my blessing or consent. Or without even so much as the courtesy of letting me know."

Theta glanced at Cracker's script again. "Well, if it's any consolation, it looks to me like he didn't let her know either. This letter was written as if she thought you knew they were married. She writes like she thinks you're going to be glad to have her visit. Good gosh, Mom, she seems to think she's going to be here a while. Oh, my gosh, I'll bet Eddie has no idea she's coming!"

May Nelle turned toward Theta, brightening. "She doesn't know we didn't know?"

"Doesn't look like it."

"Then she can't ever know we didn't. At least that will save some face. You get your overcoat on and get right over to Matthew's and have him go to the depot. Then you get right back here and make sure this place is up to snuff. I'll get to baking a pie."

"Mom, it's New Year's Eve. Matt and Judy are going out. Remember they asked me to watch the girls? I was supposed to be over there in an hour."

"Well, then, go use their telephone to call Mark to go get her."

"New Year's Eve, Mom!" Theta said in exasperation. "Everybody in the known universe is going out tonight. Except me."

May Nelle gave her The Look, the one that exuded disdain and at the same time projected an extreme dislike of Theta's words, actions, and Theta herself. "Then you'll have to go. Put on leggings. There's no telling how long you'll be sitting in that drafty depot. Stop in at Matt's to get the girls and bring them over here. I'll set them to changing the sheets on Camille's old bed."

"And you'll bake a pie?" Theta asked rhetorically over her shoulder as she reached for her thinning tweed jacket hanging on the hall tree by the door.

The walk to the depot was colder and therefore seemed longer than she anticipated. There was little wind, but the night air stung her nostrils and cheeks. Theta was glad for the leather gloves that shielded her hands as they clutched the collar of her coat where the button was missing.

If she hadn't splurged for these gloves, she'd not have come up short for a full year's tuition to Earlham and wouldn't have had to ask Eddie to loan her fifty dollars. If she hadn't asked Eddie for the loan, she wouldn't have received the letter from Cracker containing the money order. If she hadn't gotten that letter, she wouldn't have started the correspondence that developed into the easy friendship with her new sister-in-law.

And then that wouldn't have led to the poor girl's mistaken belief that May Nelle would welcome an extended visit. Cracker had just supposed that everyone would welcome her like family. After all, though, it was a reasonable assumption. She was, in fact, family.

"It's all Aunt Nola's fault! Her and those beautiful leather gloves," Theta mumbled as she sloshed through wet snow toward the red brick columns of the Pennsylvania Rail Road's depot.

Inside, Theta suddenly realized that she had no way of knowing which passenger would be her sister-in-law. She scanned the rows of oak deacon's benches to see if anyone looked as if they were waiting to be picked up. Removing the woolen scarf from her head and combing with her fingers snow-dampened bangs, Theta turned her attention to Pullman cars flickering past tall double-paned windows like an old movie strobe. The train slowed to a stop.

Still too chilled to go outside where families and friends lined the track to welcome arriving loved ones, Theta peered through the glass as passengers disembarked. Again she wondered how she would recognize her new sister-in-law. And then she knew.

As if she were stepping out of the Tivoli's movie screen came, as Eddie had said, a Donna Reed doppelganger regally handing an alligator suitcase to a porter. In her other hand was a matching train case, all the rage and quite cosmopolitan. She smiled at the colored man, exhibiting deep dimples. Warmth from generous red lips melted the porter's subservient reserve. He hurried before her to hold the door into the station.

Snow blew in with Cracker, but it wasn't the icy wind that entered with her that elicited audible gasps from the people inside. She was truly a California beauty with round hazel eyes and apple cheeks punctuated by deep dimples that recessed into puckered asterisks as she bit her lower lip, scanning the waiting room. Her coat that flowed like a cape from padded shoulders billowed over legs that, as Theta had heard Mark say about 1943's Miss America, Jean Bartel, went all the way up.

Cracker stood on tiptoe expectantly. Her sweeping eyes glistened with bright hope. No one could look away. Her energy was so profound that it was like she was a pinpoint of clarity while everyone around her was merely a Gaussian blur. She turned her head to the right and saw Theta. Eyes lighted from within, she cried in excited recognition.

"Tooey!"

Theta exhaled. Had she really been holding her breath? Hadn't everyone?

"Tooey! I'd know you anywhere!" Cracker rushed to embrace Theta, the porter following with Cracker's grip and the train case she'd dropped. "Oh, how wonderful to see you! How divine to step off that train and find you waiting. My dear, how long have you been here? Why, you're cold as ice!"

Overwhelmed by Cracker's obvious joy, Theta could barely speak. "Uh, uh . . ."

"Let's get you something hot to drink. Over there in that little coffee shop. Is your mother here, too?"

"Uh, no," Theta managed as Cracker pulled her toward the tiny restaurant tucked into a depot corner. "Just me. And I haven't been waiting long. Guess I'm still cold from the walk."

"You live near?"

"Not far," Theta lied. "But let's do have a cup of coffee or maybe some hot chocolate first. How did you know me anyway?"

"Why, the picture Eddie has of the two of you, of course."

Theta smiled, pleased.

The two were lucky to find a booth vacated moments before by an elderly couple who'd hurried into the waiting room. Watching the man and woman embrace a soldier walking with a cane, Cracker whispered to Theta, "He was in my car. A lovely young man as all our men in uniform are. I didn't mind having

150

to give up my seats on the trains from St. Louis and Indianapolis one bit. Why, a lot of these boys don't have but a few days at home before they're shipped out again. Some of them, Theta, don't even know where they're going. And neither do their folks."

She paused for breath only long enough to remove her coat. "That's the way it was with Eddie. Got called up right before Christmas, just like that. I was so lonely, I just had to come be with his family."

Theta stared as Cracker laid the cape aside but saw instead her mother's angry hand holding the letter that had inadvertently announced Eddie's marriage. May Nelle's head would have surely exploded if she'd known she'd been kept in the dark for almost two years. Well, Theta thought as she surveyed her sister-in-law's radiant magnificence, she'd know it now.

Cracker was still happily and obliviously chattering away. "He's gonna be over the moon when he finds out I came to his mama for our baby to be born. Won't he be surprised."

Theta nodded, hoping her own surprise didn't show while imagining her mother's imminent reaction to this home front bombshell.

Chapter Twenty-three

1944-45

Her Story

It turned out that Theta's dire imaginings over steaming cups of cocoa and a shared egg salad sandwich hadn't come close to the scene May Nelle made over a butterscotch pie in her rental's kitchen an hour later.

As soon as she saw her daughter-in-law's billowing coat, she suspected the worst. It was plain as day that this woman with lipstick as red and bright as new blood had seduced her innocent Eddie. She would bet money on it if she had any, because if anyone knew men, it was she, the mother of eleven. This painted hussy's temptation had obviously been too much for the boy.

"So!" she thought behind protruding eyeballs before uncontrolled words burst from angry lips. "This here is why my Eddie went and got married on me!"

May Nelle maniacally shouted numbers while counting on her fingers the months she imagined might have passed since the shotgun nuptials. Her screeches building to hysteria that neighbors two doors down could hear through closed windows, May Nelle demanded in breathless shrieks to know how long the two had been married.

She thought the answer would be shameful. But not this!

"Married two months?" she gulped, looking as if her eyes would pop right out of their sockets when Cracker held up two fingers in front of amused ruby lips.

Cracker laughed outright. "Years, Mama. Years! We been married almost two *years*!"

"I don't believe it! Eddie would never have withheld something so important from me. Why, he wouldn't. He just

152

wouldn't!"

May Nelle grabbed the back of a kitchen chair to keep herself from falling to the floor as she allowed her knees to dramatically buckle.

"Two years? Two?" she breathlessly asked.

Cracker's laughter was oddly lusty. She was tickled to witness right off the bat her mother-in-law's infamous temper along with a bonus display of drama. She'd heard accounts from Eddie, in the way of anxious explanations about why she should stay put in California this Christmas. But his pleas had only served to intrigue and tempt her.

Not surprised that Eddie hadn't told his mother the whole truth, Cracker could not have been more pleased to enlighten her. This was fun.

"Yes, ma'am," she brightly confirmed. "Almost two whole years. And it seems our boy left you with another surprise. Ya got a grandchild comin' and it's not illegitimate."

Turning the knife, she emphasized, "Not a *bastard*!"

May Nelle slumped against the straight-back kitchen chair and closed her eyes against the offense, both the profanity and the wound to her pride.

Cracker patted her bulging stomach, beaming. "Now, if ya want, I can let you in on another little surprise. On *him*! We can be friends and surprise him when I let him know I dropped in on you! We can send him a letter from all three of us. Boy, is he going to squirm!"

Her laughter was like bubbles from the twins' ornate clay pipes, filling the room with shimmering orbs of jubilation, bursting over them with shimmering iridescence.

Theta had almost raised her arms to catch the happy sounds as they bobbed and danced to the rhythm of Cracker's glee.

What kind of girl had Eddie married, she wondered. Who in the world wouldn't be upset by immediate and obvious dislike from a mother-in-law? Who wouldn't burst into tears instead of laughter at being met by such inhospitality? Theta was fascinated.

Still clinging to the chair, May Nelle wasn't as captivated by this charismatic girl as Theta had been from the moment she saw her step from the Pullman. She stood in the kitchen doorway watching Cracker be blissfully unaware that May Nelle probably never would be susceptible to her charms. Theta believed that Cracker had brought the California sun into this drab, dismal kitchen. May Nelle, though, always had pulled the blinds against sunbeams.

During all her freshman classes after the holiday, Theta felt the tickling afterglow of Cracker's happy entrance into the Whittle household. Conveniently ignoring how her mother clearly demonstrated disapproval, as evidenced by May Nelle's shouts, moans, and eventually night-long sobs that New Year's Eve, Theta had become thoroughly mesmerized by her sister-in-law's gay, forthright personality. She'd never witnessed anything like it and wondered at the unlikely match Cracker made with her somber, stoic brother.

As she hurried down the women's walk at Earlham College toward the Old National Road to catch her bus, Theta also wondered how Cracker got through the long days with her mother. Gripping the loose collar of her coat and holding it with both hands over her ears against the March wind, she imagined what the two of them might be doing right now. Her mother in the overstuffed chair leaning on one elbow toward the window to get a better view of their neighbors' comings and goings; Cracker lumbering after Mark and Georgeanne's twins as they wreaked havoc with curious little hands.

"Thank You, God," Theta said aloud, meaning it. "Thank You for sending Cracker to help Mom. Thank You I got on nights at the Harvester. Thank You for giving me the strength to stand up to Mom when she said I couldn't work and go to school too. Oh, God, thank You for that!"

Two girls passed from behind on either side, hurrying toward the bus stop. Theta didn't care that they may have heard her talking to herself, she was so relieved to be out of her mother's house for the better part of every day. She chanted her mantra. "Thank You, thank You, thank You."

Coming toward campus on the other side of the drive, on the men's walk, was a heavy-set man walking as if pushed from behind by the wind. There were less than a hundred men enrolled at Earlham during wartime, so she knew all of them at least by sight. This one was familiar, but she didn't recognize him exactly. He didn't look like a student; they were either old or unfit for service. This one seemed young and healthy. Maybe a conscientious objector visiting the Quaker campus while on leave from a military staff assignment. She couldn't help but rudely stare, unable to quite place him.

"Gosh, he looks just like Junior," she mumbled, narrowing her eyes to better bring him into focus. Before reason could overrule impulse, she blurted, "Junior!"

The man looked her way, frowning. "Theta?"

"Why, Junior, it *is* you!" Theta hurried to her country cousin and crossed the drive to the men's walk, ignoring the Quaker campus rule separating the sexes. She grabbed his arms, bringing him close for an embrace though he flinched and pulled away. "What are you doing here?"

"Looking for you."

"For me? I mean, what are you doing in Richmond? Why

aren't you in Europe?"

"Got shot. Here." He pointed to his left bicep.

Theta's delight turned to concern.

"But Theta, that's not why I'm here." He looked at her with sympathy that pierced her heart. Alarmed, she felt a sting in her chest that rose to her throat and at the same time dropped to her stomach.

"Mom."

"No," he shook his head. "Gilbert."

Theta's relief was so immense she exhaled a high-pitched cry. If he'd just come right out and told her something had happened to her mother's brother, she would have been immediately concerned for the poor soul. But with her first thought being dread for her mother, the blow was softened to nonexistence.

"What happened? Is he okay?"

Junior shook his head. "He's dead, Theta. I come to tell Nola and your mama. Daddy said it wouldn't be right to call on the telephone with news such as this."

Theta nodded, ridiculously thinking they didn't have a Bell anyway, even though she was making a good wartime wage.

"So I come up to tell y'all. I'm real sorry, Theta. Nola said I should come get you on account of your mama's takin' it real hard. I'm supposed to carry you home right as soon as I found you."

Theta shook her head to clear it. "I can't. I'm working second trick at the . . . at a munitions factory. I catch a bus out here and go straight there from class every day. I gotta go or I'll be late."

"You cain't miss? Even if it's on account of a death in the fam'ly?"

"Well," Theta said slowly, "I guess I might. I guess I could maybe go see the foreman about it. Hurry, or we'll miss the bus."

Junior put his arm around her shoulders and turned her toward the National Road. "I got the Ford. Daddy give it to me to come tell y'all. I sure am glad I told Nola first. She's with your mama and that lady. Who is she anyway? Looks like a movie star. Or would if she wasn't . . . if she wasn't . . . uh."

He looked at his feet, embarrassed.

Theta smiled, hugging his unwounded arm. Relieved, Junior guided her to the dilapidated pickup parked on a side street across from campus.

"Your mama was abed and at first didn't understand it was Uncle Gilbert that was dead. She acted like she was sorry and all but then right away summoned that girl to fetch Nola and me some dope like we was on a social call. She a hired girl or something?"

Theta laughed at the backwoods word for Coca-Cola. "No. She's Eddie's wife."

"She sure is purty. Just like Eddie to go and get him a purty one. Wonder Gilbert didn't tell us nothing 'bout her."

"He was gone before she got here, so he didn't know Eddie was even married. My brother Peter ran Gilbert off one night when he was sleeping at our house on account of the cold, even though it's none of his business anymore. You'd think he still pays the bills."

"Yeah, we figured something like that happened when Gilbert showed up at our place. It was colder'n a billy when he come a-knockin'. He looked like a tramp. Must've took him a couple weeks to make it."

"He's been living with Aunt Shirlee and Uncle Honey all this time?"

"Since just before Christmas. He wasn't no trouble. He was good at heart. Just cain't hold his liquor. And that's what done him in."

Theta nodded as she opened the creaking door to her cousin's rusted Ford and slid onto the brittle seat cracked with age. "I guess I shouldn't be surprised."

The truck sputtered to life with the help of a few choice words from Junior.

He looked sorrowfully at Theta. "Haint the drink overall what prob'ly done it, Theta. It was some bad wood alcohol some sorry sumbitch give him. Or sold him more like. If Daddy ever finds out who, there'll be hell to pay. We found him a-laying in the ditch down the lane. At first, we thought he froze to death. But then we seen the bottle of 'shine."

"Does my mother know?"

"Not about how we found him. Nola said not to tell her. We're supposed to say he died in his sleep. No, your mama took it hard enough as it was."

"What happened? You said my mother didn't understand it was Uncle Gilbert. What happened after that?"

"Well, when Nola told her about Gilbert a-dyin', your mama said real funny-like, 'that's too bad' then told Eddie's wife to go get us some dope. Then she went to telling us about her chest cold like there wasn't nothing more important. Nola didn't have no patience for that and told her again about Gilbert. Only this time she said, 'our Gilbert.' Your mama got to lookin' like she was going to have a stroke and said, 'my brother?'

"Good Lord, Theta, I haint never heard screaming like that in all my life. Like to give me the shivers."

"Oh, Junior," Theta said. "Please hurry."

That night, lying in bed with her mother, Theta closed her eyes tight trying to shut out the sounds of May Nelle's grief.

"He had so much promise," his sister gasped over and over. "So handsome. So young."

There was no comfort for May Nelle that night or the

following day or week. She took no interest in the commotion of Cracker leaving for the hospital after bloody water gushed onto the kitchen floor from under her skirt. Not even Nola could rouse May Nelle from her bed to go see the new baby in Reid Memorial Hospital's nursery.

The old woman laid in natal anguish until Cracker returned several days later with her infant son, named for his father. May Nelle's whimpers quelled only when she heard through her agony the newborn cries coming from somewhere inside her house.

She raised her head to listen, her eyes intently trained on her closed bedroom door. "Gilbert?"

May Nelle insisted on holding the baby nearly all of his waking hours, rocking her torso in the overstuffed chair by the front room window as she cradled him. She coddled and cooed to the consternation of both Theta and Cracker.

"Gilbert. My sweet babydoll Gilbert."

Chapter Twenty-four

1945

His Story

Smiles dutifully dated his letter in the upper right corner as June had requested after receiving multiple letters at once and being unable to determine which he'd written first.

"March 11, 1945. Dear Junie: I got six letters from you today! We're anchored off an island and so got mail call this afternoon. Just as soon as I got off duty, I came down to my bunk to spend some time with you."

He'd gotten several letters from Grace, too. They were lying unopened beside those from Mom and his mother. He'd read their letters after June's, saving the newspaper clippings that both women included of local news, sports, and obituaries of people they knew but of whom he had no recollection. He might read some of those carefully cut out articles after he finished the letter to June, if only to stall some more before guiltily turning to Grace's mail.

The onus he felt at not being honest with her was the same disturbing emotion that kept him from opening her letters. More powerful than guilt was his fear that he would hurt her with the truth. If he read her letters he'd have to write back.

He lifted one of June's lavender envelopes and breathed in her perfume. He was suddenly awash with the conviction that he was also being dishonest with June. That did it. He'd write Grace tonight to break off with her. He couldn't stand a liar. "And that's what I am," he said aloud, pressing June's envelope to his nose, breathing in the L'Aimant he'd given her for Christmas when he was still in Norfolk.

"Yeah, I won't even read her letters," he said to himself,

satisfied that he'd made a good and right decision. "I'll just write and break it off easy."

But when he opened his eyes, he was looking straight at the Woolworth envelopes that contained Grace's faithful letters, and he lost resolve.

Smiles gathered her unopened envelopes and tucked them into his undershirt. He'd take them up to the fantail later and read them there. Somehow, he rationalized, reading them in the open air rather than in the privacy of his bunk seemed less distasteful. Less like he was hiding something. For now, he didn't want to think about anything but June.

He picked up his pencil stub and continued writing. *"Thank you for spraying the perfume on your letters. Reminds me of that last Christmas with your folks and how after you opened that bottle, you pretended to put some behind my ears. It reminds me of how you put kisses there instead and how we sat on your porch swing holding hands almost all night long. How soft your hands are. When I hold your letters, I'm holding your hand."*

He paused, unconsciously scratching his stomach. Grace's letters! Sight unseen bugging him. Smiles eyed the bulge under his white cotton shirt inches from the letter he was writing. He lifted the makeshift lap desk of this month's *Stars and Stripes* and set it aside. He wadded the unfinished letter to June and tossed it with disgust into a mound of wadded candy wrappers at the foot of his bunk. Trying to rid himself of unsavory guilt, he gathered June's letters and placed them under his pillow.

He hopped off his bunk grazing Watkins in the bunk below.

"Hey! Watch out there, will ya, Smiles? I'm catchin' some shut eye in case we get liberty on Ulithi. You oughta get some, too, and go with us this time."

"*If* they give us liberty," Smiles said without making a commitment as he ducked past rows of bunks.

"Hey, wait a minute," Jim called. "Where ya goin'? To see the show?"

"Naw. *A Song to Remember* doesn't sound like my kind of movie," Smiles called back as he paused before ducking through the hatch. "Besides, it's almost eight o'clock now. Wouldn't make it in time."

"So where ya goin'?"

Without thinking, Smiles put his hand over the bulge above the waistband of his naval dungarees. He took a deep breath. The letters beneath pointedly accused dishonesty. Exhaling in a rush he invited, "I'm headed to the fantail for some fresh air if you want to come along."

"Yeah, sure."

The two had just stepped through the portal when they saw Kelly coming their way. "Where y'all headed?"

"The fantail," both answered with identical jerks of their heads in invitation.

The three walked single file through the narrow passageway, Smiles in the lead. Stepping through another portal, they approached the mess. Smiles glanced in as they passed. He'd taken only a few steps beyond when he stopped so suddenly Kelly stumbled into him. Smiles leaned back, stretching to see into the dining hall. Mumbling excuses he squeezed back past his two friends. He ducked into the mess and anxiously scanned the room.

He was sure he'd seen someone he'd known a long, long time ago.

A group of sailors sitting at a far table were playing cards. They were surrounded by kibitzers but otherwise the mess was empty. One man facing the doorway saw Smiles and waved him over. "We're playing euchre and need a fourth to get up another table."

His eyes intently searching the room, Smiles said, "You see a fella, oh, about eight foot tall in here a minute ago?"

Several card players laughed, exhaling clouds of smoke. "Eight foot tall?" one said. "Yeah, he was over there by Harvey."

The card player laughed anew coughing phlegm. Squinting his eyes through the smoke from a Camel hanging from his lips, another sailor slapped down a card. "That aint funny, Mac. Here, Smiles, come sit in for me, will ya? I gotta go to the head."

Smiles was still searching the room for the colossal man. He nodded, and reluctantly Kelly and Watkins followed as he crossed the room toward the card players.

"Hey, I thought we was going up to get some air," Watkins said over Smiles' shoulder. "What you talking about some eight foot guy? Is that what you seen in here?"

"I just thought I saw somebody I hadn't seen in a long time. I was a kid at the time and he seemed big to me."

Smiles took his friend's chair. A swab standing off to the side shuffling a deck of cards like he knew how invited the other two to join them. "How 'bout a friendly game of 21?"

"Nah," said Kelly unconsciously jingling the change in his denim pants pocket. "We're goin' up to the fantail for some air. We're gonna be headin' out as soon as the guy gets back from the head. Right, Smiles?"

"Go ahead and play some 21," Smiles said, dealing another hand of euchre. "We can go up later."

"You sure?"

Smiles turned up a Jack of clubs and glanced at the lineup of five spades he held in his hand. He nodded at Kelly, then studied his cards, trying his best to appear stymied. His partner peered through a swirl of Camel smoke at the five clubs in his hand and knew that Smiles had dealt him a loner. He began slowly, "Oh, go ahead and pick it up. I guess I'll go al . . ." when a deafening

163

blast rocked the Randolph along with a jolt so intense that the men looking on stumbled into one another then onto the table before landing on the hard linoleum.

There was a moment of stunned confusion, sailors looking to one another for an explanation.

"We been hit!" someone yelled.

They helped each other gain footing and rushed to the passageway. Thick black smoke heavy with oil forced them back to the mess where they shut tight the metal portal door. Above them they could hear wailing sirens and megaphone orders to attend general quarters. Within moments the mess became an oven. They turned their eyes overhead, grimly realizing a fire must be raging above.

Though they'd only stepped a few feet into the passageway before being forced back by the cloud of black smoke rushing toward them like the gush of water from a main break in a sewer tunnel, their faces and clothes were black. One by one they peeled soiled shirts from their sweating bodies. Grace's letters fanned through the air along with Smiles' denim work shirt and undershirt, landing helter-skelter among spilled coffee and shards of broken Coca-Cola bottles.

Smiles headed to the galley with his shirt in his hand. He ran cold water over it, not bothering to wring it out. He wiped his brow, then tied the shirt around his head. "In here!" he called.

He stationed himself at the sink and soaked each man's shirt as it was handed to him. Stopping only to slip his belt from his pants' loops to use as a tourniquet around the arm of a severely bleeding sailor, Smiles drenched shirt after shirt. The heat in the mess was unbearable. Steam rose from the makeshift turbans almost as soon as they were wrapped around the sailors' heads. Eventually, Smiles used a galvanized mop bucket to pour cold water over his friends' heads and bodies as they lay nearly naked on the galley floor. It was with unexplainable strength that he lifted weighty bucket after bucket, splashing contents over the men until water ran two inches deep over the dining hall floor.

Lounging on a raft in the Ulithi lagoon, Dick Tiernan watched, horrified, as a twin-engine kamikaze bomber slammed into the fantail of the USS Randolph's starboard side. He looked at his watch: 8:07 p.m. His mother had written him that Smiles was aboard the Randolph.

Helpless to do anything else, he prayed.

Chapter Twenty-five

October 1945

His Story

Smiles thought he'd already lived through his worst nightmare. Twenty-six men were killed the night the kamikaze dove nose first into the fantail of the USS Randolph. One hundred and five sailors were injured. There was no telling how many more might have been lost or wounded had the movie theater not been letting out the audience from its first showing, as more sailors were going in for its second.

For sure, there would have been three more deaths had Smiles not thought he'd seen the unusually large, strangely familiar man in the mess on the way to the fantail. As it was, he was trapped with more than a dozen men for four hours in the stifling galley.

Ever since, Watkins and Kelly had tailed Smiles wherever he went. They were convinced, as Watkins had unabashedly confided to him, that he was "too good to die."

The two sailors believed that if they stayed near him that they, too, would be protected.

"What was it, anyway," Watkins continually wanted to know, "that give you the strength to keep all us guys from roasting to death in the galley that night? And what about that guy you think you seen? The one that made you go in there in the first place. Somethin' just don't seem natural to me. What was it give you the strength?"

Watkins was asking Smiles the same question as the Randolph entered the Port of Norfolk. "C'mon. Ya gotta tell me. I can't go on wonderin' the rest of my life."

Scanning the crowd on the naval pier, Smiles gave his friend the same answer he always did: a shrug. He was looking for June amid what looked to be half the female population of the Commonwealth of Virginia, when he saw with horror what his parents had surely thought would be the surprise of his life. They were right.

Standing on the dock, waving madly over their heads as the Randolph rocked slowly to a stop against the wharf were Mom, Pop, his mother and father, and Grace. Unaware that she was standing just behind them was June. The ship, Smiles thought, couldn't progress slowly enough to spare him the devastation of what lay ahead.

He never recovered Grace's soggy, oil-stained letters from where they landed after he stripped off his shirt and undershirt in the searing heat of the ship's mess. The next day, when he had a chance to sit down, he wrote his parents about the kamikaze hit. Though he omitted details, he discovered that he couldn't write about the attack more than once, so asked his mother to let everybody else at home know he was okay. He decided this might be a good way to break things off with Grace. He didn't answer her letters, but now and again asked his mother to pass along his regards.

June read of the kamikaze strike in the *Norfolk Daily News* and had seen grainy footage taken from Ulithi in movie theater newsreels. She chastised Smiles for neglecting to mention the attack but reassured him in letter after letter the following six months that she continued to wait alone for him on the swing of her parents' front porch.

She kept the promise she made before he left, and she was keeping a new one, too: waiting for him on the pier when he returned home.

Too soon, he was face to face with not only June but also his folks, and Grace. All raced to embrace him. Smiles drew Jacky

167

into a bear hug so strong it was as if he didn't want to let her go. Chuckling, she stepped aside as his grandmother wrapped her arms around him. Mildred, reluctant to release her grandson, pulled Grace into their embrace. Looking over their heads, Smiles saw June standing back. Having guessed that these were his grandparents, parents, and one of his sisters from Indiana, she seemed pleased, her tickled eyes crinkling over a broad smile. Her white gloved hands excitedly squeezed the straps of a leather pocketbook smashing the front of her skirt as she waited to meet her new family.

Smiles swallowed and said as he reached a hand toward June, "Hey, everybody, I want you to meet somebody real special."

June took his hand, allowing herself to be drawn into a hug that nearly left her breathless. She raised on tiptoe to kiss his cheek and leaned coyly into his shoulder as she smiled at the startled group. Smiles wished the ground would open and swallow him whole but continued with the same bravado that carried him through many a tough jam.

"This is June Hert," he pronounced. "June, this is my grandma, Mildred."

"Mom!" June said, grasping Mildred's hand in both hers. "I've heard so much about you!"

Smiles continued the introductions. June took each one's hand in the semicircle, thrilling his grandfather Gordon and father Porter with kisses on their cheeks. Finally, Smiles came to Grace. Her grin not faltering, June asked brightly, "Would Grace be Presh or Sis?"

Grace giggled, but Smiles said solemnly, wishing now that he'd written that letter breaking it off with her, "Neither. This is a friend from back home."

He meant to get across the platonic nature of their

relationship, truthfully presenting Grace as a family friend. But his nervous introduction, as well as the way Grace beamed at Smiles as if he alone stood on that crowded pier, gave away the complete truth.

For only an instant June wavered, her smile frozen. "How nice to meet you, Grace."

Turning to Smiles, she said too gaily, "What a lovely su'prise fo' ya, Smiles! I guess you won't be needing Daddy's cah aftah all. He sent me oveh with it just as soon as he heard y'all's ship was comin' in. Tol' me to carry ya on oveh home. Well, now I guess I jus' got a su'prise to tell him instead!"

She purposefully checked the dainty gold Bulova on her left wrist. "Oh my goodness, it's latah than I thought! I gotta be runnin' along. So glad to see ya back safe, Honey."

Liquid eyes peered into Smiles' pained ones. "I jus' *know* Grace is."

"Don't go," Smiles said, unsuccessfully reaching for her elbow as she turned to leave. Grace claimed June's vacated spot beside Smiles and possessively slipped her arm through his.

June ignored the gesture as she pulled the Lincoln's keys from her purse. She said in a rush, "I'm so glad to have met y'all because, you see, I'm goin' down to Mobile for a coupla days an' I woulda hated to have not met y'all. Please fo'give me for runnin' off. Oh, my, I jus' got so much to do.

"I'll jus' be runnin' along now," she trailed as she threaded her way through the smothering crowd.

Smiles called after her, "I'll call."

June turned, glanced longer than necessary at Grace's hand clutching Smiles' bicep before smiling with the poise so common among Norfolk belles. "No, Smiles, theah's no need fo' that."

Chapter Twenty-six

October 1945

Her Story

"I know what let's do for Halloween," Cracker said, absently twisting a length of wet blonde hair around her index finger and securing it with a hairpin against her scalp. "Let's us go have our fortunes read!"

"What for?" Theta asked, sitting on the edge of Cracker's unmade bed, her chin cupped in one hand supported by one knee crossed over the other. "You're going home to Eddie soon. You've got little Eddie. You already know your future. And I know mine, too. I'm here with Mom. Past, present and future."

Cracker blew air around a hairpin clutched between her teeth, blowing off Theta's cynical excuse. "You don't hafta be. You're going to college, aren't you? Nobody but her says you can't have your own life. And seems to me, you've done made that move."

Indignant, Theta said, "Eddie went to college, why can't I? Never mind, I know why. Because it's always, and always has been, Mom's excuse: *He's the boy.*"

Cracker was defensive. "He had an athletic scholarship. You're spending good money on college. And not a state school like Eddie, either, but that expensive private one. Why in the world would you choose to stay here in town and waste money on Earlham tuition?"

Theta plopped backward onto feather pillows piled against the bed's headboard, demonstrating her resignation rather than irritation. "And then who'd take care of Mom? Camille's living with her Jimmy's parents, and Marlene's sure not going to come home from the bright lights of New York to take a turn."

She sighed and curled an arm under her head to better see Cracker as she wound another strand of hair around her finger. "Mom seems to think I'm going to quit school. She's just waiting for me to give up working and going to college at the same time. She doesn't have any idea how hard it'd be for me to get a good job without a diploma. Especially now that men are coming back to claim their jobs, and factories have lost their war contracts. You've been good to chip in some of Eddie's pay. But you'll be gone soon."

She flung her other arm over her eyes to shut out the only future she could envision. "To tell you the truth, after all the men come home, I don't see how Mom and I are going to live til I graduate and start teaching."

"Oh, quit being dramatic, Theta. When you act like that, especially with that dowdy hairdo and not a smidge of mascara, you look just like your mother."

Flushing with anger, Theta wanted to scream at Cracker, "At least I have a relationship with *my* mother." Instead she ignored the intended insult and returned to the subject. "It's not easy, but I feel I'm doing the right thing. That's what really counts. Besides, if I'm true to loyalty, I have no other options but to finish college and get a good job in order to sufficiently take care of her and me."

"And I."

Theta didn't debate whether or not to correct her sister-in-law. That particular grammatical gaffe was a pet peeve. "No, Cracker. It's 'me.' You wouldn't say 'take care of I' would you?"

Cracker ignored her and shrugged. "You can do what everybody else does; get married and let him support you."

She blithely twisted a strand of nearly dry blonde hair around her finger then let it fall into a lazy spiral before taking it up again. "Of course you'd have to date to do that."

"I've dated. I went to my senior prom."

"I'm not talking ancient history, Theta."

Cracker tied a scarf over the mass of pincurls, smiling into the dressing table mirror. "It's despicable that Mom doesn't let you date. It's just not fair. You have a life and she shouldn't tell you how to live it. She's selfish."

Theta closed her eyes to shut out the disloyal truth of Cracker's words. "I could date if I wanted to. There just aren't enough men to go around yet. And when they do come home, oh boy, the competition! Good luck."

"Here's what you do," Cracker said, turning on the three-legged stool in front of the dressing table. "This works every time. You fix your eyes on the fella you want. Don't stare at him. Just sorta look sideways at him from under your lashes. Like this."

Theta laughed at the sight of Cracker, the tight scarf covering her head, tilting her chin downward and looking at Theta from under half-closed lids laced with dark lashes. Lauren Bacall beckoning Bogie. Her mouth was pressed tight with the corners only slightly lifted into a coy smile. Her dimples were deep.

"Got your attention? That's the hook. Now comes the reelin' in." She winked one eye and turned back to the mirror.

"That's it?"

Cracker nodded, obviously pleased. "Uh huh.

"You stare at somebody until they notice you, wink and then turn away?"

"That's right."

She spit onto the mascara block in its tortoiseshell case and stirred with a tiny brush before applying more goo to her lashes. "Except you don't stare. You study him like you're interested, but only so-so. Almost like you've got something better to do.

He'll feel your eyes on him. As soon as he looks at you, wink. Real quick. Then turn away. Heck, you don't even have to reel him in. He'll swim to you and land floppin' right at your feet!"

"That might work for you. But I don't think I could ever do anything like that. Even if I had the chance. Right now I've got to figure out how I'm going to finish college."

The room was quiet as Cracker concentrated on lengthening her lashes. Theta watched transfixed.

She brightened. "You know who keeps me going every time Mom brings me down? Aunt Nola. I've always wanted to be a strong, independent woman like she is. Since I was a little girl. I love her so much. She always encourages me. Like, you know that short story I worked so hard on? I put my whole heart into it; I've never worked so hard on anything in my life.

"When it was finished, I wanted someone I respected to read it and tell me what they thought before I handed it in. So, I gave it to Aunt Nola to proofread. I knew it was good because when she gave it back to me there wasn't a mark on it. And she said how proud she was of me and how much she liked it."

Cracker quickly said, as if she'd been waiting for the chance, "She didn't really like it. She just told you that. But she told me it wasn't good at all."

The unnecessary barb pricked like a saber, even though Theta doubted Aunt Nola would say anything of the kind. She'd witnessed Cracker's cruelty many times. She had, in fact, ignored other hurtful comments aimed at her or her mother, delivered in the same off-hand manner. Over the past months, Cracker's charm had exponentially faded for Theta with each airy insult. Now, at last, she saw her sister-in-law with fully unclouded eyes. Selfishly mean.

Still, the heaviness in her heart wasn't just a new contempt, it was also a new thought. *Why do I love her? Cracker doesn't deserve my devotion.* Theta was for the first time conflicted about Eddie's wife. She abhorred her, but she loved her. She was certain that this lovely woman had, in the ugliest of ways, meant to hurt her. And yet she hoped that what she believed was not true.

A smug smile exposed Cracker. Theta realized with an unhappy jolt that it was indeed true: Cracker was pleased to have wounded her to the core. Worse, she was elated to have hit her mark. Theta knew by Cracker's compressed lips that she was controlling the urge to laugh aloud. As she'd often done, Cracker adroitly maneuvered the topic away from her intentional attack.

She flippantly said, "You do need to go have your fortune read. C'mon; let's go."

Following Cracker from the room, Theta somehow had the gumption to limply protest. "It was a good story. I got an A."

The dollar was dear. Theta wished she could be as cavalier about spending as her sister-in-law was. Cracker pulled money from her wallet as if it were confetti to be thrown into thin air.

"Come on," Cracker said, tugging Theta's arm. "You walked all the way down here. Don't back out now."

The two were standing on an uneven sidewalk outside a frame house in a rundown neighborhood on the city's far south side. A hand-lettered cardboard sign behind a filmy window leaned against faded curtains pulled shut against curious eyes. It proclaimed the house's occupant to be a "Fortun Teller."

"She can't even spell, Cracker."

Cracker sighed her disapproval of Theta's skepticism and left her sister-in-law on the sidewalk. She stepped onto the crumbling cement stoop to knock at the door, and said loudly as if Theta couldn't hear her, "Good Lord. The poor thing thinks college makes her smart, but you can't learn common sense."

Theta and her friends at Earlham had heard this before. She smiled, remembering what Sue had said. *"Ever notice everybody who says this doesn't have much education?"*

Quizzical eyes peered from a small naked window in the door. Cracker waved the dollar and the door opened. A middle-aged woman in a worn chenille housecoat ushered her inside, then beckoned Theta with a stern wave of her hand. Theta looked to her left and right to make sure no one could see her before she hurried up the crumbling front walk. If she weren't still too polite to abandon Cracker as she knew she should, she'd turn tail and run from the house, its seedy neighborhood, and the narcissist being ushered inside.

"Sit here," the woman ordered crossly, motioning to a low couch covered by a quilt that'd seen better days.

Though it was against her better judgment, Theta obediently sat. Perched on the edge of the stained couch and its inadequate camouflage, she warily watched the woman guide Cracker into a nook just off the front room. There were no curtains separating the two rooms. Embarrassed, Theta pretended to study the opposite wall. She couldn't help but hear cards being shuffled and Cracker instructed to cut them. She then heard the slapping of individual cards onto what appeared to be a sheet of plywood covered by a fringed shawl lying across two sawhorses.

"Ah," she heard the woman say ominously before the rest was lost in a harsh whisper.

The reading took only a few minutes. But from the look on Cracker's face, she didn't mind. "You're next!" she enthused, pulling Theta from her precarious seat.

Theta saw with curiosity that the woman had the same wiry gray hair as the other fortune teller from so many years before. There was no crystal ball here, but the feel was the same. Dark, sinister. She remembered Junior's foreboding as she'd pressed him to go with her to see the Gypsy at the Jefferson County fair. She had been too excited then to care. Now, she felt ashamed. And a little afraid.

Sensing her discomfort, the woman laid aside her cards and studied Theta's face. "I can tell you right now. I don't need no cards to know your future. You want to know?"

Theta nodded, clenching the secondhand alligator purse in her lap. The woman impatiently motioned with the fingers of her right hand for the required dollar.

Snatching the money before Theta could push it across the table, the woman said with brusk confidence, "You're gonna be married within the year."

The two women stared at one another. The fortune teller sharply nodded her head at Theta, a sign that the session was finished. There had been no cards, no reading of Theta's palm, no leaves in the bottom of a teacup. Just one short sentence. Theta couldn't help herself. She laughed.

Relieved to be hurrying down the fortune teller's front walk, trying not to think of the dollar she'd left behind, Theta laughed again.

So did Cracker. "Married within the year! You'd have been happy if she'd said you'd be dating somebody within the year!

"But you were right," Cracker conceded. "What a waste of money. She told me something stupid, too."

Cracker leaned into an unusually frigid Theta to keep the late October chill from penetrating the ballooning frayed maternity coat. "Did you hear what she told me?"

Theta shook her head.

"Well, it doesn't matter. It was ridiculous anyway."

"Oh, no you don't. You know what she said to me. What'd she tell you?"

Cracker said disdainfully, as if she knew there may be some

truth to the reading, "She said I was a bridge burner and I had broken someone's heart. She said this person had adored me so I'd be forgiven, but soon the relationship will be ruined all the same. That crazy old woman said I would do it over and over all my life. 'Burning bridges' she said. Old coot."

Theta wondered how the old lady knew, but instead said, "Well, this is what the fortune teller really told us: we both wasted our money. Who could ever help but always adore you?"

She was still thinking of the impossibility of the fortune teller's predictions while running to catch the bus for her weekend job selling movie tickets at the Tivoli Theater downtown. Theta rummaged in the bottom of her purse as she ran. She hoped there would be some coins caught in one of the corners and was sorry she didn't have that dollar she'd wasted earlier. Just as she and the city bus simultaneously reached the stop, she found a dime lying amid gritty lint, a small bottle of Jergen's Lotion, and a half stick of Black Jack.

Nearly out of breath, she managed to smile at the bus driver as she handed him the coin. From the back of the bus she heard someone call her name. Looking up, she saw Grace Wettig waving to her in the friendliest manner. Grace was kind and pleasant, but Theta knew her only as someone she'd seen around with Smiles. She waved back tentatively, not sure why this Fairview acquaintance wanted her attention. Still, as the bus lunged onward, she made her way to the empty seat next to Grace. She'd barely settled in beside her before a stack of photographs was shoved into her hand.

"I just got these developed," Grace enthused.

Theta pretended interest, beginning to shuffle through the small black and white images framed in scalloped white. "What are they?"

"Kodaks of my vacation to visit my boyfriend."

The photograph in Theta's hand showed a grinning sailor leaning against an Oldsmobile next to two older men and women. He seemed to be looking straight at her. Theta would recognize that smile anywhere, even though she hadn't seen Smiles since talking with him about the election three or four years before. Had it really been that long?

"I know him. He goes to my church. Where are you?"

"Taking the picture."

"No, I mean, where was the picture taken? Where'd you go on vacation?"

"I went with his parents and grandparents to meet his ship coming back from the Pacific. This was taken at Virginia Beach."

Theta's heart jumped. The postcard from Sue so long ago! She slipped the photograph to the bottom of the pile with her thumb, suddenly interested in the rest of Grace's pictures. The next had Grace in it. She and Smiles were lying beneath a beach umbrella in the sand, a series of ocean waves beyond them. "Was it red?"

"No. It was a maroon suit."

Realizing she'd blurted her thought about the umbrella, Theta covered her embarrassment by nodding. "Pretty."

"Sort of, but not really my style. I had to borrow it from one of Smiles' friends. A real sweet girl. I didn't know it'd be warm enough to go to the beach, so I hadn't packed a bathing suit."

"He has a girlfriend in Virginia Beach? I thought you said he was your boyfriend."

"I mean a girl from the family he knows there. Her name's Peg. Really Marguerite, but she goes by Peg. She's like a sister. Here we are at their house having a picnic. And here they are, all except one daughter who was out of town. And here's one of

Smiles' mother and grandmother wading in the ocean. Look how they're tiptoeing into the surf. Aren't they both just darling? You should have heard them giggling."

Theta slowly shuffled through the photographs, listening to Grace's exuberant descriptions, carefully studying each one and imagining herself in the scenes. She sighed wistfully. "You're so lucky."

"I know. Isn't he handsome?"

Theta returned to the photograph of the two older women. Their dresses were lifted above their knees as foam from a retreating ocean wave washed over bare feet and ankles. Though their heads were bent toward the salty spray, their faces hidden, they were obviously howling with laughter.

"Yes, he is" Theta agreed, smiling at the image of the laughing mother and daughter. "But I mean I wish I could go on a vacation like that.

"With people like that."

Chapter Twenty-seven

November 1945

Her Story

Camille opened the wrought iron gate to her mother's front walk just as the Western Union boy was knocking at the door. She walked with a leaden pace toward sure tragedy while at the same time fumbling for a dime in her coat pocket. The boy and trembling young woman made a silent exchange. Camille read the name typed onto the envelope, gasped, and opened the door. Her eyes fixed on her sister-in-law's name, she nearly bumped into Theta, who'd heard the boy's rap.

Camille thrust the wireless toward her sister. "It's addressed to Cracker. Should we open it? I think it's okay, don't you? But you look. I can't."

All May Nelle's sons who'd been in the war had come back home. All except Eddie. In fact, they hadn't heard from him in what seemed like ages though it'd only been a couple weeks. Neither had Cracker, that they knew of. Theta, her face grim, slowly raised her hand to take the message from Camille. Inhaling a deep breath, she turned the envelope over to slip a fingernail beneath the flap.

She exhaled in relief. "It's for Cracker, all right, but it's from her sister, not the Army."

"Read it!"

"Oh, Camille, I can't. It wouldn't be right."

"But maybe she's saying something about Eddie."

Theta turned to hurry upstairs where Cracker was napping with Little Eddie. "Cracker! Cracker! You have a telegram!"

By the time Theta and Camille reached the landing, their sister-in-law had opened the bedroom door. "What's it say? Oh, give it to me!"

She swiftly read the telegram, then dropped it to the floor. "I've got to pack. My mother's died!"

"Oh, Cracker. I am so sorry," Theta said.

"What can we do to help?" Camille asked.

"Get my bags from the attic. I've got to get there! I have to go. Right now!"

"Of course you do," Theta said sympathetically. "I'll get your grips."

Cracker, holding a palm to her forehead, pushed past her. "I'm going to run over to use Judy's phone. I've gotta call the depot. Please let there be a train home this afternoon!"

As she clattered down the stairs, Cracker's voice trailed back to her sisters-in-law though she seemed to be talking to herself. "Oh, I've just gotta get there before my sisters strip the whole house. And they know Mother's jewelry belongs to be me!"

Camille turned open-mouthed to Theta, her eyes querulous.

"Yes, you heard her right," Theta said with a sigh. "This does it. I've lost all respect for her this time, Cammie."

"What do you mean? Surely, she's just in shock. She didn't mean it."

"Oh, yes, she did. She's gotten two letters telling her that her mother didn't have long to live. I couldn't understand how she could know her mother was dying and not go. I know it's a long way, but . . ."

"She knew and didn't go?" Camille stated what was obvious but hard to understand.

"Not until there was an actual death and there was something in it for her."

She may have opened Cracker's telegram, but it wasn't like Theta to open her mother's mail. But the writing on the envelope, though it had no return address, was Cracker's. With both twins down with chicken pox, May Nelle had gone to babysit at Georgeanne and Mark's. Theta looked at her watch. She couldn't wait another two hours until her mother returned to see what Cracker had to say. They hadn't heard from her since she'd left three weeks earlier. Eddie had written he was back in California but had said little else. Theta decided to go ahead and open the letter herself. Maybe Cracker was writing something about Eddie or Little Eddie.

"Anyway," she rationalized, flipping shut the rusty mailbox lid, "this is probably for me, too."

Theta tapped the envelope on her palm, sifting the paper inside to the bottom. She carefully tore it evenly along the edge as her mother always did then pulled out the two-page letter and unfolded it. At first, she was surprised it was written on lined paper rather than Cracker's signature delicate stationery. She made a note to start writing her letters on the paper she usually reserved for schoolwork. Anything Cracker would do had to be in vogue. If Cracker didn't use stationery, neither would she.

She dropped her books on the end table then plopped on the davenport before taking off her coat, already beginning to read what appeared to be hastily scrawled thoughts. *"May Nelle,"* it began abruptly.

Theta's eyebrows narrowed. She sensed this letter was not meant for her to see after all. Its tone, from the acutely frosty salutation, was disturbing. She looked to the bottom of the page to see the signature. *"Nanette"*. This time Theta's eyebrows lifted in surprise. It was from her sister-in-law all right, but not signed with the affectionate nickname. Disturbing indeed.

She knew she should put the letter back in the envelope, but she couldn't stop now. She started reading from the beginning.

"May Nelle,

How can you stand yourself? You are a lazy busy body who lives off the backs of your children. How dare you write us and ask for money? You said we owed it to you since Eddie didn't take his turn. Whatever that means. Well, I say we already paid you enough. I gave you half of Eddie's pay while we lived with you and even if I didn't, I worked off my 'rent' taking care of those two brats. All you do all day is sit in that chair and be in everybody's business. And you order that poor Theta around making her do your work. That poor girl is going to be a spinster because you have made her weird. No wonder she doesn't have any friends and had to hang on me day and night."

Theta suddenly felt as if she'd been punched in the gut. Though she'd already lost all respect or admiration for her sister-in-law, her twisting and turning stomach was crowding upward to press against the heart miserably breaking above it. With shaking hands, she brought the letter close to her face and read on.

"As far as getting money from Eddie, forget it. I can't believe you'd even ask. Didn't Camille or Marlene want to give you anything? Or didn't you ask them? I guess you think Eddie is going to support you now that he's got his Badge Pay. What about all those other sons? Did you go to their well once too often and they're sick and tired of giving you money? We have our own family to take care of. You can't expect us to be supporting you and Theta."

Feeling nauseated, Theta looked to the second page. She could hardly believe Cracker had more to say. Obviously, she was on a roll, and that wasn't all. The cursive becoming scribbles was clear evidence that her loathsome anger was viral.

"You need to start working yourself. If you didn't sit in that chair all day maybe you wouldn't be so heavy. Get up and get working. We don't owe you anything. I already did my share so

Theta could go to college. If it wasn't for me babysitting and doing your housework, she would have had to stay home and do it. I know you wouldn't lift a finger! I didn't appreciate being treated like a slave. You already have one."

Theta gasped. She knew Cracker meant her. Through angry tears, she squinted to decipher the last paragraph.

"I can just see you telling Eddie what I said. Well don't bother. He wouldn't believe you over me. I'm sending you this letter because he's going to be sending you money and that isn't right. You have caused trouble between us and I guess that just makes you happy. But don't you dare ask for any more or I'll make sure you never see him or Little Eddie again. By the way, his name is not Gilbert.

Nanette"

Theta could hardly breathe. She scanned the letter. Certain words popped off the page to slap her in the face. *Weird. Slave. No friends. Hang on me day and night!* She didn't want to read them again. She knew she didn't have to. Those words would surely stay with her for a long time. Probably forever.

She thought of Cracker's other haunting words. *She didn't really like it . . . she told me it wasn't good at all.* And the insinuated insult to both her and her mother: *without a smidge of mascara, you look just like your mother.* Cracker's laughter the night of the fortune teller reverberated: *Married within the year! You'd have been happy if she'd said you'd be dating somebody within the year!*

Theta crushed the letter in her fist. "This bridge is burnt! This is probably why she came here instead of staying with her own family. I bet she'd already burned that bridge. This is the kind of thing she must've written in those letters she asked me to mail when she first got here," Theta said aloud through furious, hiccoughing sobs.

"No wonder she never heard from anybody back in California until they asked her to come home before their mother died."

Suddenly she had a guilty revelation. "I should've seen it. Cracker did show me how hateful she is! She was always saying bad things about Mom behind her back, but I just didn't care because I was usually so mad at Mom myself. And she said things about me, too. Right to my face! And I let her do it."

She began to sob anew. "And to think I thought she was beautiful."

Theta laid her head against the back of the davenport, closed her eyes, and cried, trying to squeeze the pain from deep within. After a few minutes, with the back of the hand holding Cracker's letter she wiped tears from her cheeks. *How in the world can someone I have no respect for hurt me so? I guess I must still love her. Damn loyalty.*

Feeling sorry for herself wasn't a new concept for Theta, and it wasn't unusual for her to build impotent anger against her mother or sisters. So, it was easy to hurl rising anger in Cracker's direction. For the better part of an hour she slumped on the couch in her worn coat, wiping tears from the corners of her eyes. Like her tears, though, her anger gradually began to wane and finally still.

Theta realized with a shadow of self-resentment that she had adored Cracker too much to let this change everything she meant to her. She knew, though, that her sister-in-law would never again be beautiful in any way. She couldn't help herself from hearing May Nelle's voice lecturing, *Pretty is as pretty does.*

She looked at the crumpled letter in her hand. It embarrassed her as if it had corporeal power. She picked up the envelope from the floor and carried it with the balled paper to the kitchen. She lifted a wooden match from the tin hanging on the wall above the gas range and struck it. She dropped the letter in the sink and held the flame to it.

Using a crusty soup spoon, she rolled it around in the sink until only a delicate blackening disc remained and the fire licked upon itself until it too was ash. Determined that the ugly words be destroyed, she ran tap water over the charred feathers until they dissolved and swirled down the drain. The envelope lay beside the sink. Taking it up, Theta tore it in half again and again until the layered bits were too dense for her to tear. She carried the offensive trash to the garbage pail and pushed the tiny squares deep into the slop.

"Gone," she said, wiping her hands on the dish towel hanging by the sink.

Eddie's letter with a cashier's check for thirty dollars arrived in the next day's morning mail. Her mother was sitting in the overstuffed chair by the front window when Theta handed the envelope to her along with a cup of tea and triangles of cinnamon toast. She sat on the couch waiting, hoping that Eddie was characteristically brief. "What's he got to say, Mom?"

May Nelle handed the letter to Theta. "Not much."

"What's that?" Theta asked, pretending that she didn't know the paper her mother had folded and slipped into her dress pocket was Eddie's check.

"Your brother has sent us some money." May Nelle said.

She withdrew the cashier's check and handed it to Theta. "You may as well deposit this in the bank on your way to school."

Theta took the check then turned her attention to Eddie's letter. Written in pencil, it was indeed brief.

"Mom. Here's thirty dollars to help you and Theta until I can get more to you. You don't need to ask any more. I'll try to

186

send something every month until Theta graduates. Again, no need to ask. Your son, Eddie."

Theta looked at the check then at her mother wiping sugar from the corners of her open mouth with a middle finger and thumb. "Mom, I've been thinking. There's just two of us now. That upstairs is just going to cost us money as winter comes on. Why waste heat? You and I share just the one bedroom down here. I've always wanted to live in a little apartment like Aunt Nola. Why don't I look for one? It'll save us money on rent and maybe I can find one close to Earlham that'll save me bus fare."

"Well, I've been thinking, too," May Nelle returned in a tone that begged a fight. "If you quit that college maybe you could get on days at the Harvester and keep that night job at Howell's. That and your ticket sales down at the Tivoli would keep us all right. Nobody else in this family 'cept Eddie seemed to think they needed a hoity toity degree."

Narrowing both her eyes and eyebrows, Theta was ready for this fight. She tapped Eddie's check against her cheek. She appeared to be thinking, artfully buying time as she eyed her mother taking a sip of tea.

"This check here," she began after May Nelle replaced the cup on the saucer and leaned toward the spotless window to watch a passing neighbor.

"This check here," Theta continued in a voice that sounded calmer than she felt, "I'm going to send it back."

May Nelle abruptly turned her attention from the window. "You will not!"

"Yes, I think it's the right thing to do. Eddie has a wife and child. They're sure to have another one on the way soon. It's just you and me here. There's no reason I can't keep on at school. I've only got one more year after next semester. If we move into an apartment, I'm sure we can make it now I'm back at the jelly

187

factory nights and still selling tickets on weekends."

"Oh, Theta Marie, that's ridiculous. You can't support us on two part-time jobs. You need a good day job. How will we live? What would we eat?"

"We can do it. I don't eat much anyway and with just the two of us, our grocery bill isn't high. I'm going to look for a little one bedroom or maybe studio apartment right after class today."

"You are not," May Nelle said with finality.

"And," if she could have held her breath and still speak, Theta would have. But she took a deep breath and continued. "And you need to tell Mark that if he wants us to keep the boys while Georgeanne works, he'll have to begin to pay us just like he would if he sent them to the day nursery."

"Why, I will do nothing of the thing!"

Theta stood and crossed to her brother Peter's old desk. Pulling a slip of note paper from a drawer, she picked up a fountain pen and wrote, *"Dear Eddie, thank you so much for this check. But Mom and I have discovered we can make it on our own. Please buy something nice for Cracker with it. Love, Tooey."*

She took a stamp from the roll, licked it, and placed it on the corner of an envelope. As she addressed it, May Nelle shouted, "What are you doing? You give that check to me right this instant, young lady!"

Her back straight as a ramrod, Theta placed the check and note inside the envelope and licked it shut. "I'll be back late today, Mom. I'm going to look for an apartment after class. It's up to you what you do or don't say to Mark about paying you for babysitting. Just keep in mind that you like your sweet rolls."

Calmly shutting the front door behind her, Theta smiled. It was the first time she'd ever stood up to her mother. It felt good. It felt right.

After dropping the envelope containing the uncashed check at the post office, Theta stopped at Woolworth's to buy a newspaper. Sitting at the soda fountain counter, she sipped a glass of water as she perused the classifieds. This would be tougher than she thought. Evidently the men returning from war had caused apartments to be few and far between. And more expensive to boot.

"You wanna order something?" the waitress asked, pointing to Theta's water glass.

Theta looked at the girl's pencil poised above a pad. "No, thanks. But I'm wondering . . . I sell tickets at the Tivoli on weekends. Since it's so close, I'm wondering if maybe there's any openings here on Saturday and Sunday nights after I get off from there?"

The waitress assessed her as if weighing possible competition. Finally she pointed with her pencil. "See that guy over there? Go talk to him."

Anyone else's heart may have been heavy, leaving Woolworth's with yet another job. Not Theta's spirits. She felt light as a feather, her shoulders so unburdened by worry of how she would keep her mother's household afloat while earning a degree. A good teacher's salary would free her from struggling the rest of her life to make ends meet on usual women's wages.

"I'll be free of a lifetime of monotonous piece work," she crowed unabashed as she stepped onto Main Street's busy sidewalk from the five-and-dime. Then her shoulders perceptively slumped as she remembered other circumstances.

"If not free from Mom's thumb."

Chapter Twenty-eight

November 1945

His Story

It was the second morning in a row that Smiles sleepily stumbled into his mother's kitchen and saw that he had his choice of not only a mixing bowl full of warm tapioca or a lemon pie high with toasted meringue peaks, but also a farmer's breakfast complete with sides of fried potatoes and grits. He laughed aloud at the thought that his mother had valiantly tried to replicate the grits he'd told her Pearl served alongside bacon and eggs.

"What's so funny?" Jacky asked.

"How long's this going to keep up?"

Jacky poured a cup of strong black Maxwell House and set it on the kitchen table. "You've only been home three days. I can spoil you all I want for as long as I want. Now pull up a chair and sit down."

Smiles set a spoon in his cup to draw off the coffee's heat then reached for the oleo. He may have developed a taste for grits but hadn't accepted that in the South it tasted just fine without butter flavoring or sugar. "I'm going down to the Hoosier Store later on for a new suit. Need anything while I'm out?"

"Why in the world do you need a new suit?"

"Well," Smiles began, then hesitated while he stood to pull Jacky's chair from the table for her, "I think I need to go get a job before all the other fellas snatch 'em up. There's gonna be a lot of competition, even with a lot of guys taking Uncle Sam up on his G.I. Bill and going to college."

Though it'd been nearly ten years since Porter had given up

drinking, his long-ago taunts still drove many of Smiles' decisions. He could clearly hear his dad's repeated refrain of "dummy" whenever he thought about his future.

"College isn't for me, Mother. But I don't want to go back to the Malleable, either. Or the Crosley."

"What are you thinking you want to do, then?" Jacky asked, spooning sugar into her coffee. "Doesn't seem to me there are many choices unless you want to try over to the Avco or something."

"I want to be a policeman," he said with finality.

"Oh!" Jacky said, surprised.

Smiles laughed. "I've put a lot of thought into it, Mother. So I'm going to go get a suit then head straight to the City Building to apply. I ran into Mayor Meadows yesterday downtown, and he thought it was a grand idea."

Their conversation was interrupted by banging on the back door to the tune of *Shave and a Haircut . . . two bits!* The caller didn't wait to be invited in.

"Just in time!" Louie cried, his hungry eyes taking in the feast set before Smiles. Grabbing a plate from the cupboard, he reached for the pie before he'd taken a seat.

"Save some for Mom." Smiles grinned, shaking his head. "And me."

Nodding thanks to Jacky for the cup of coffee she set before him, Louie said with a full mouth, "How 'bout coming with me and the fellas to Earlham around four o'clock? Take a look at some of those co-eds."

"Can't. I'm going to get me a suit this afternoon then apply for a job."

"A job?" Louie asked. "We hardly got home. What's your rush?"

"I want to get hired while the hiring's good."

"Where at?"

"Police Department. Gonna get a suit then stop at the City Building."

"A policeman, eh? That doesn't sound half bad. Say, let's go see us some girls at the college this afternoon, then go tomorrow. That'll give me time to get my graduation suit cleaned so I can go with you.

"And," he waggled his brows, "first things first."

The Men's Department was on the first floor at the Hoosier Store. Entering from Main Street, Smiles looked past fashionably wide ties in a case to his right then saw a rack of ready-made suits beyond it. He stood before the row, considering the black and navy-blue suits prominently displayed. He slowly pushed aside with his right hand shoulders of the dark suits, carefully judging each one according to its weight and hue. This was his first purchase as an adult. His first suit.

Smiles stopped at a brown tailored jacket with accompanying trousers. It seemed to him to be set apart from the smart black and blue coats. Its appearance was unassuming, muted compared to the others. Smiles raised a worsted wool sleeve with a dangling tag. He raised the label to better view the price. Astonished by the cost, he dropped the sleeve like a hot shell casing.

"Good looking suit," a voice came from beside him.

Smiles changed his expression before turning toward the voice. He was already smiling with his hand extended when he saw that it was the Hoosier Store's owner, the father of one of his high school classmates. "Mr. Bartel! How's Clayton? Home yet?"

"Hello, Smiles," Emmett Bartel said, heartily shaking his

hand. "Good to see you home, safe and sound. Clayton's fine! He was in charge of over a hundred men on a supply ship in both theaters. As soon as he's ready, I plan to put him in charge of sixty employees here."

Emmett lowered his head, smiling, slightly embarrassed. "I guess I shouldn't brag."

"As Will Rogers would say, 'It ain't braggin' if it's true,' Mr. Bartel," Smiles assured.

"Thanks for that, Smiles. Can I help you find something?"

"No, that's okay. Thanks anyway. I'm just looking."

"At suits, I see. You'd make any one of these suits look like a million dollars."

Smiles didn't comment what he was thinking; that these double-breasted suits already looked like a million dollars, and to him, so did their price.

"I was just looking for something to wear for a job interview. Thought I'd start here."

"A good place to start. Let's see how one of these suit coats looks on you."

Smiles knew that the price of every one of these suits was at least double what he was prepared to spend, but he couldn't say no. He chose the brown suit and shrugged into the jacket Mr. Bartel held for him, then allowed himself to be guided to a tri-view mirror. He wagged his shoulders until the jacket fit just right.

It sure did look swell.

Smiles weighed the cost of the suit against the mental image of himself standing in front of the chief of police, asking for a job that may very well be in the hopes of a dozen other veterans. He turned to view the fit of the back in one of the side mirrors. He turned again to the middle mirror. *Boy, oh, boy.*

"Smiles, these suits are going to be on sale next week,"

Emmett Bartel said. "I don't want you to miss out on an early interview, with so many men looking for work these days. Let me mark this suit down right now."

Emmett Bartel withdrew from his gabardine jacket pocket a fountain pen, unscrewed the cap, and slashed through the printed tag. He began to print "Sale price 10," then changed it to "25% off."

Taking the jacket and replacing it with the trousers on the wooden suit hanger, he began to walk toward the cash register, Smiles following. Emmett paused and turned to his son's friend.

"Young man, if that job doesn't work out, there's always a place for you here."

Smiles viewed his reflection in the Hoosier Store's plate glass window as he passed by in the light of the midday sun. *Sure does look sharp*, he thought. He smoothed the single-pleat trousers and patted the breast pocket into which Mr. Bartel had tucked a pocket square.

Adjusting the new tie again, he set off toward the Doran Bridge that spanned the gorge, with Fairview on its other side. He'd planned to carry home the suit in a large paper sleeve made to fit new purchases but decided to wear it out of the store. It was just the thing to wear to Earlham that afternoon. *Impress the girls.*

He'd just crossed the bridge, turning onto Sheridan Street toward home, when he heard shrill screaming. A woman in a faded shirtwaist, clutching an apron to her terrified mouth, stood on the sidewalk, looking to the third story of a brick apartment building. She screamed again and pointed to a window high above, appealing to the small crowd surrounding her.

"My little girl! She's still in there. She was taking a nap. I was only gone a minute. Somebody help her!

"Mona! Mona!" she screamed through her apron.

Smiles sprinted toward the group on the sidewalk. Housewives and a few men shaded their eyes as they stared at the narrow windows of the third floor. Following their terrified stares, Smiles saw thick dark smoke belching from broken glass.

He dropped the sack holding the clothes he'd worn to the Hoosier Store and ran to the weathered front door of the burning building. Opening it, he was engulfed in choking smoke. Though he was relatively sure there were stairs leading to upstairs apartments from the first floor's narrow hallway, he couldn't see them. The smoke was so dense, he knew there was not a chance he could reach the first flight, let alone those leading to the second and third floors.

Without thought, as if guided, Smiles ran to the side of the house. There was no fire escape, but there was a trellis with withered rose vines still clinging to diamond-shaped cross hatches between two narrow frames. The trellis' legs were planted into the ground, its top bar nailed to the house's overhanging eave.

Ignoring sharp thorns, now brown from autumn frost but still threatening, Smiles grabbed hold of the trellis and began to climb. His weight caused it to bow and crack, but he swiftly put one foot above the other, pulling himself upward with hands bleeding from minute cuts of razorblade thorns. Near the top, the trellis was secured between two windows. Smiles considered briefly which to try.

The back one. She's probably in a bedroom. His decision was nearly instant. He leaned as far as he could, then reached toward the back window's sill. Clutching the peeling sill with fingers gripping the edge, he swung his legs over and hooked one foot on the sill while breaking the window glass with the other. Smoke bellowed out the newly broken window. Pulling himself up with both hands and feet, he rolled into the room.

Smiles could barely see inside, the smoke was so thick, but he had a feeling it was the little girl's room from the dolls strewn across the floor. One was a Shirley Temple, its plastic eyes a vacant stare. *Remember her name? Sure you do.*

"Mona? Mona, where are you?"

There was no answer. He crawled past the dolls toward the far wall, keeping his face as near the floor as possible. When he reached the far side of the room he groped for a bed. Not finding one, he searched unseeing for a closet door, his hands feeling along the floorboard. He hoped she was in her bedroom and had not tried to go down the stairs or into another part of the apartment.

"Mona?"

He heard crying and followed the sound to a closed door. He reached up and turned the knob. The door opened and there was a child who looked to be around three years old crouching just inside. Her eyes were wide with fear. Tears streamed down her face.

Smiles spoke in a quiet, playful voice. "There you are. What a good girl!"

He reached out his hands, welcoming her to come into his arms. She didn't move. He smiled and said, "Your mommy is waiting outside, Mona. Let's surprise her and go down the trellis. Want to climb down and surprise her?"

Mona solemnly nodded her head. Auburn hair mussed from napping bobbed in ringlets around her face. She opened her arms and Smiles locked her in a firm embrace while trying his best to be gentle as he slid her from the closet. Shielding her from the smoke, he tucked the little girl beneath him as he crawled toward the broken window.

With his right elbow he knocked jagged edges of glass from

the frame and ran the sleeve of his new jacket around the exposed edges to make sure they were smooth and wouldn't cut the girl still gripped in his left arm. He lifted Mona onto the ledge and once again gripped her in one arm before sliding down the trellis, his other hooked around one rail, as if it were a fireman's pole.

Near the ground several men waited with lifted hands. He safely transferred Mona, who had begun to wail as she spotted her mother, into the men's arms. Jumping to the ground, he heaved a relieved sigh then quietly disappeared unnoticed around the front of the burning building.

Entering his kitchen from the back door, Smiles found Jacky leaning over the stove. She stirred gravy in a cast iron skillet with one hand, the other on her hip. A familiar sight. She turned with a smile that quickly devolved into alarm.

"Good Lord, Smiles! What in the world happened? That suit is a sight and torn to shreds."

Inspecting the worst of the sleeves, she said again, aghast, "Good Lord!"

Smiles put his arm around his mother, kissed the top of her head, and whispered, "Good Lord is right."

Chapter Twenty-nine

November 1945

Her Story

In literature class that afternoon, Theta tallied household expenses and tuition against projected income from working weekday nights at the jelly factory, weekend days at the Tivoli, and now weekend nights at Woolworth's. Then there would be the refreshment stand money come summer.

The figures were heart-stoppingly close, but slightly ahead on the right side of the equation. "I can do it," she mumbled, her stomach tight.

"Huh?" Sue whispered.

Theta glanced at her friend and shook her head. She silently mouthed, "Nothing."

She looked back at the figures peeking from under Dante's *Divine Comedy* and smiled at the irony. "Nearly nothing."

After class, Sue nudged her. "Hey, old friend, now that you don't have to hurry off to make artillery guns or whatever it was you were doing to nip ol' Hirohito's keester, how about coming with me and Helen to the Dugout for a Coke?"

Considering the need to preserve the meager coins in her change purse, Theta shook her head. Besides, she'd defied Mom enough today already.

Then she remembered Cracker's ugly but inspiring words. Without giving another two thoughts to the cost of a Coke or her mother's already ignited ire, Theta changed her mind. *I do have a friend! Two of them. Maybe I'm not weird after all!*

Or a slave.

Theta followed rather than accompanied Helen and Sue to the Student Union basement where her classmates often met for study groups and socializing. In nearly three years at Earlham, she'd never been to the Dugout. She imagined it to be quiet as a library, but when she entered behind her friends, she was surprised to find it teeming and chaotically loud with a cacophony of cheerful voices.

"How on earth do you study in here?"

Helen and Sue laughed. Sue put her arm around Theta's shoulders. "Put on that famous smile. Haven't seen it in years."

Theta grinned, embarrassed, remembering her high school experiment. "I was such a baby."

"It worked, as I recall. Hey, let's get a Coke and try to find a table. Gee whiz there's a crowd here today."

"It's those Army and Navy boys back home and checking out the coeds," Helen correctly observed.

Theta glanced around the room. Helen was right. There were dozens of men in obviously new or outgrown civvies standing in groups, most nursing Cokes in six-ounce glass bottles, laughing somewhat awkwardly at their own jokes. Some had ventured to talk to girls with books under their arms or on tables. In the center of the room, Theta saw Eddie's old Fairview friends. They surrounded their reunited gang leader, whose broad laugh strained buttons on what appeared to be the same white shirt he'd worn to church years ago.

"There's Smiles Smythe!" Helen said.

"Hey, good lookin'!" Sue said under her breath. "What I wouldn't give . . ."

Theta blurted, "I know him."

The other two stared at her in disbelief.

"I do. We go to the same church. Remember, Sue?"

Helen and Sue sighed with disappointment. They turned away, each searching the room for a vacated table.

"I'll bet I can get him to come over here," Theta said quickly, suddenly confident.

Successfully regaining her friends' interest, she lowered her chin and languidly gazed at Smiles from under her lashes. It didn't take nearly as long as she'd thought. Like Lorelei and a sailor too long at sea, Smiles turned his head to meet her eyes. Imitating Cracker, Theta flashed a wickedly crooked smile and winked. Immediately, as Cracker had instructed, she turned attention back to her two astonished friends.

"Don't look so flabbergasted," Theta laughed. "You'll scare the poor boy awa . . ."

Smiles was already standing beside her.

Chapter Thirty

1945-46

Her Story

His pick-up line wasn't in the same league as her come-hither. "How's Eddie? Has he come home yet?"

With Sue and Helen eagerly looking on, Theta hoped Smiles would flirt with her. She didn't have any idea how that might be, but she was fairly certain it didn't include asking about her older brother. Maybe, she thought, she didn't look as attractive giving the wink as Cracker would have. Maybe it was just a coincidence that Smiles had come over just at that time, only to ask about Eddie.

"He didn't get hurt or anything did he?" Smiles asked, looking concerned by her hesitation.

"Oh, no, he's all right. He's in California, married and a father. I don't guess he'll be coming back here. Any time soon, anyway."

Smiles nodded as if he were considering Eddie's current status. He moved his eyes slowly around the circumference of the Dugout and then back to her. "Say," he said, "I haven't seen you at church since I've been back."

"We don't live in Baxter anymore. We're over on the east side now. It's a long walk."

"Oh. Well, then, how about if I pick you up in the car this Sunday?"

Theta didn't know what to say. She was almost twenty-one, after all, and didn't need Eddie's friends ferrying her about.

Sue nudged her. "That would be nice, Theta. Weren't you just telling us how much you missed church?"

Theta was looking at her shoes as she nodded, embarrassed

to think she'd made a fool of herself in front of the whole Dugout.

Sue leaned toward Smiles to be heard above the din. "She lives right across from Starr School. On the corner."

"Okay, Theta?" Smiles asked. "Pick you up at 8:30?"

Theta could feel Sue poking her in the back. She looked up at Smiles, took a deep breath and smiled as if she didn't feel ten years old and two inches tall.

"I'll be ready," she said brightly.

"See you then." Smiles gave each girl a grin, lingering on Theta's flushing face then turned to rejoin his friends.

Theta turned to her own friends. "Why'd you do that, Sue? I'm not a kid. He's going to show up with Grace and I'll be sitting in the back seat with his little sisters."

"His little sisters? You mean Presh and Sis? They're married! Besides, you dope, he just asked you for a date."

Theta, who'd turned her back in the hopes that Smiles wouldn't see the embarrassment rising in scarlet blotches over her cheeks, looked over her shoulder at the group of laughing boys from Fairview. "He did?"

The following Sunday Smiles showed up at 8:30 on the dot. She was ready, sitting in Mom's chair by the front window, and hurried out the door before he was halfway out of his father's Oldsmobile. Mom, who'd been in a snit ever since Theta had gathered the nerve to tell her she'd be going out this morning, was still in bed.

Theta heard May Nelle pathetically call as she shut the door, "Theta Marie, how can you leave when you know I'm so sick? You may just come home to find me de . . ."

Smiles guided Theta to the sedan with his hand lightly pressing into her lower back. She'd never experienced such a sensation. That effortless touch possessed inordinate power. She wasn't sure if his hand remained on her back as he leaned to open the passenger door for her. The slight pressure seemed to be still on the small of her back, but so was a slight nudge on her elbow as Smiles held open the door.

Sue and Helen had been right; neither Sis nor Presh were in the back seat, holding the seatback forward so Theta could slip in beside them. Smiles was guiding her to the front seat. The empty front seat.

Maybe Helen and Sue were right about Smiles' intentions, too, Theta thought as he gently closed the passenger side door then winked at her as he crossed in front of the Olds. *Is this how dates work? Shouldn't I at least know for sure?*

After church, Theta had no choice but to accompany Smiles to his grandmother's for Sunday dinner. It was understood. And that's when she understood that indeed, she was on a first date with her childhood crush.

After a riotous Sunday dinner attended by what seemed to Theta half of Fairview, Smiles dropped her at her job at the Tivoli Theater. He had to scurry around the back of the Oldsmobile to help her from the car. Theta had already opened the door herself.

Embarrassed by her obvious gaffe, she blurted a thanks and hurried across the sidewalk. His hand was still extended, suddenly empty. Smiles could only mumble a perplexed goodbye. Theta couldn't see his amused, crooked smile as she rushed inside. She was just sure this morning's trip to church and family dinner had been her first and last date with Smiles Smythe.

Her heart sinking more with each thought, Theta replayed the morning as if it were the film being shown directly behind her ticket booth. There was a cloud over her mind that overshadowed any sensible response to every little comment thrown her way throughout the morning at church and then at the family Sunday dinner. Smiles' friends showed no pretense of politeness, and their careless banter made little sense to her.

Crimping the ends of several tickets on the roll to make them easier to detach, Theta hummed her familiar song. "I don't care; I don't care . . ."

What she did care about was how Smiles' parents and grandparents must be feeling about her. The love around the Flaugherty's dining room table was palpable. Theta was surprised and delighted by easy kisses that passed between her date and the women who raised him. She stopped humming, remembering the laughter she could not, by any might, muster to join. They must think her at best dull. Thinking what worst must be, Theta dropped the roll of red theater tickets and covered her eyes in an attempt to hide from the dreadful thought.

By the time Theta got home from Woolworth's that night, May Nelle was in such a state of disbelieving fury she had made herself indeed sick. While Theta had been in a torment of embarrassment, her mother had been having worse imaginings. Despite more than two decades of grooming, Theta was not the meek and devoted companion that was to have been her destiny. She was, of all things, a college student ripe to liberal thought. She was running after boys. She was, this very day, in the clutches of that Fairview ruffian. Oh, she knew what he was, and didn't like him one bit.

May Nelle pounced before Theta had time to push shut the front door. "Theta Marie, you were not raised this way. I cannot believe all the work I've done to mold you into the young lady you should be has been so disregarded. I have sacrificed and sacrificed. Yet here I sit alone while you're out chasing after men. Your schemes are scandalous."

"We went to church, Mom. And then to his grandmother's for . . ."

"His grandmother's house? Oh, Lord, he's settin' you up to take your wages and put you to workin' in his kitchen and . . . and . . ."

"Mom! Nothing of the kind. It was Sunday dinner with his family. There were his parents, his sisters, their husbands, a couple of his friends and us there. My gosh, Mom,"

Theta headed for the room she shared with her mother. "And right after dinner he took me to the Tivoli to sell my tickets. This was probably a one-time thing. So don't worry about that."

"So, why was you so late gettin' home?"

"Did you forget I work at Woolworth's of Saturday and Sunday evenings now?"

May Nelle harrumphed, still not convinced she wouldn't be sitting alone in poverty the rest of her life.

Despite Theta's social ineptitude, or maybe because of it, Smiles made it routine to pick her up from Woolworth's every weekend night. He then would sit well past midnight at the Whittle's kitchen table eating bowlfuls of popcorn, causing May Nelle to suffer weekly migraines. Theta maintained her grades, her three jobs, and a strict curfew that left no time for actual dates.

Still, May Nelle fumed. Theta steadfastly refused to stop seeing this maddeningly cheerful home crasher. Though she missed the days when she could retire after hearing the 11:00 p.m. news on WKBV, May Nelle wouldn't dream of leaving Theta alone with that man for one minute. She maintained watch from her overstuffed chair by the front room window where she could keep an eye on the goings-on both outside and in. Particularly in her kitchen.

"I can't stand a liar," Smiles was saying. "And I found out that when you hold back the truth just to keep from hurting somebody's feelings, well, that can cause all kinds of problems."

Smiles unknowingly multiplied May Nelle's ire by tipping back the kitchen chair in the crazy way boys do. Eddie had often sat at the table this way, balancing on the chair's hind legs. But that was different. Smiles took Theta's hand across the scarred kitchen table.

Ignoring the showy disapproval from the next room, he continued, "That's why I hafta tell you that I'd been seeing someone pretty seriously before we started keeping company. Down in Norfolk. And so . . ."

"I know," Theta said, unable to mask in her voice the fatalistic surety that Smiles would tire of the constraints imposed by May Nelle, her responsibilities to and for her mother, and her own shortcomings, which she was certain were plentiful.

She withdrew her hand. "Grace showed me the pictures she took in Virginia Beach."

Smiles ignored another May Nelle harrumph. He put his hands in his pants' pockets, looking relaxed though his expression was pained. He rocked the chair back and forth, reminding Theta of Aunt Shirlee and Uncle Honey. She rose from the table, took up the new aluminum popcorn bowl she'd splurged to buy just that evening from Woolworth, and tried with more stamina than she felt to walk with erect dignity to the sink.

Smiles watched that straight little back, hating what he was about to do. "No, not Grace. That was over a long time before she came to Virginia. That's what I mean. I lied to her when I didn't break it off after I got serious with a girl down in Norfolk."

He brought the chair back to its four legs with a thud against the linoleum and rushed, "That's why I hafta tell you where I'm going tomorrow."

Theta turned slowly from the sink. She thought her heart would shatter into piercing shards, sure he was breaking it off with her to go back to Grace. Now she felt stabbing fear under her belt. This, she thought, sounded worse.

"Where are you going?"

"To Norfolk for a few days."

The fear bounded from her stomach to her chest where it left a searing pain before it lodged in her throat. "To Norfolk? To see . . ."

Smiles nodded, his eyes downcast, his lips uncharacteristically tight.

Chapter Thirty-one

1946

His Story

From the looks of it, the neatly folded letter could have been a pack of Pall Malls. Smiles reached into the breast pocket of his dress shirt and brought it out. He'd read it, he guessed, a hundred times. But maybe he missed something. He unfolded it, leaned back against the Pullman backward-facing seat, and brought the fragrant stationery to his nose. He closed his eyes and breathed in deeply.

He couldn't remember the name of that perfume but recalled with satisfaction the joy he felt when June had opened the Christmas present then playfully sprayed him. Sniffing the aroma clinging to the stationery, he felt the calm it'd brought him on the aircraft carrier after mail call; but also the pain when he read her old letters after she refused to see him anymore.

He began to read this latest missive. *Dear Smiles.*

The words were blurred as if she'd sprayed too much perfume on them, but he could easily read the few short sentences. *"I don't know if I can forgive you. But I can't stop thinking about you. Did I make a mistake? Should I have given you at least a chance to explain Grace to me? It just doesn't seem like you to be a two-timer. I am mad at myself and wonder if maybe I should give you that chance to explain. I'm leaving it up to you. I'm sure you have a stamp."*

Smiles could have used a stamp but hadn't. Instead, he boarded the first passenger train from Indiana to Virginia. As soon as the Norfolk and Western pulled into the Norfolk depot he hailed a taxi and went straight to the Hert's house. June opened the door, her mouth and eyes wide with surprise when she saw Smiles standing on the other side. It'd been just four days since she mailed her letter.

"I guess you've come to 'splain," she said, standing aside.

How he loved Virginia Beach. Even in Norfolk, a half hour from the Atlantic, Smiles could smell the ocean. Salty, fishy, inexplicably fresh. But here on the beach itself, his bare feet plodding along the wet shoreline, he didn't have to breathe deeply to take in that signature aroma. The atmosphere itself was gloriously heavy with it.

June was skipping ahead of him, her espadrilles swinging from her right hand. While his toes sank deep into the moist, grainy sand, he could see from the vanishing imprints that hers barely made contact. *She's such a dainty, tiny thing*, he thought, not for the first time.

"Oh, look!" she called, stopping to point beyond rolling waves. "Dolphins!"

Smiles caught up to her and shaded his eyes to locate the playful porpoises. He laughed. "I could live here. This is paradise for me."

"You know you can, Sugah. What's stoppin' ya?"

Smiles hesitated. June put both arms around his waist and squeezed.

He scanned the ocean. The dolphins had disappeared. He could see to the horizon, a different hue of blue ever darkening toward space. The waves rolled uninterrupted toward shore, rhythmic and mesmerizing until they rose up to crash down against sand beaten as hard as cement. The foamy remnants creeped toward his feet, gently tickling his toes before receding back into the surf.

Smiles sighed and bent his head to kiss June's soft curls. He raised thoughtful eyes to scan the distant, cloudless skyline. "I love this place. It's bee-u-tee-ful."

A decision made, he said, "Let's go have a Coke on the boardwalk."

Chapter Thirty-two

Summer 1946

His and Her Story

His photograph, the one taken in his sailor suit just after he enlisted, was still turned to her bedroom wall. Theta was too mad to look at it. She was determined to not moon over that handsome nineteen-year-old face topped by a GOB hat barely holding dark blond curls from his smooth forehead. She would not, absolutely would not, long to kiss those full lips broadly encompassing straight, even teeth. That smile. She refused to look at it.

In fact, she refused to have anything to do with him. Why his likeness, displayed in an art deco black-and-white glass frame, remained atop the dresser she shared with her mother was beyond her. She couldn't stand it. Yet, she could not bring herself to throw it away, or at the very least hide it in a drawer. It made no sense.

It wasn't as hard as it might have been had the image of Theta's determined walk from the kitchen, her head held high, not kept invading his every thought. In his mind Smiles saw her straight back, proud with control, against the backdrop of everything he loved about Virginia Beach. He saw it now even as June delicately sipped her Coke through a paper straw.

Smiles had been in Virginia only a few days. That's all the time it'd taken for him to know that his heart was back home. Home in Indiana with Theta. Despite a lingering fondness for June, he couldn't stop thinking about Theta. She was a spunky little thing, shy as she was, and with so much to overcome.

June raised laughing eyes from her Coca-Cola.

"I've been dating someone back home," he said abruptly.

Smiles thought he was returning to the girl he'd first seen with the bobby pin holding back mousy bangs from a forehead too large for her face. He expected to be greeted with the reticent smile Theta reserved for her happiest moments. But when she opened the door to his knock after he'd rushed back to Indiana, she met him with a wicked grin.

"It's nice you're back, Smiles," she said from inside her front room, the screen door still between them. "I prefer the quiet, though. It's much nicer being alone with Mom. Yes, much nicer. I like it better with just Mom and me."

"I came straight from the depot . . ." he began.

Without giving him a chance to finish, she shut the front door. She didn't slam it. But the click of the lock was firm.

Over the next several weeks, he stopped again a few times. She was never home to him and he, at last, couldn't again face her mother's smug, conqueror's contempt.

He tried to talk with her at the Tivoli ticket booth, but Theta wouldn't acknowledge him or curtly instructed him to step aside for customers. He haunted the Springwood concession stand, still wearing his policeman uniform following his shift, but she lifted her chin to stare beyond him.

Francis was still dating Sue, so Smiles resorted to asking for his old friend's intervention. "No dice," he was told, in somewhat different phrasing, but not nearly as firmly as Theta had already pronounced.

"Helen," he asked the moment she answered the phone, "what can I do?"

She knew. "Nothing. There is not a thing you can do to make up for hurting her the way you did. All her life she's felt unwanted. You hammered that nail but good."

"What'd I do?" He honestly didn't know.

"Well, for starters, you let her know in no uncertain terms that you were still interested in that girl from Virginia Beach. After leading poor Theta on."

"That's not it at all," he said, confused. "I just had to make sure. It's not that I didn't want Theta. Just the opposite. I needed to make sure I wasn't being blinded by how much I wanted to live the rest of my life with her. 'Cause, you see, I kinda thought that about June before."

"Well, that's helpful," Sue said sarcastically. "Sure would make me feel better to know you weren't sure, so you had to go see your other girlfriend. Boy, oh, boy. That's rich."

Smiles saw her point but had to be truthful. "Well, yeah. I had to go see June to know. I came back, though. Doesn't that count?"

There was a pause on Helen's end of the line. Then a sigh. "Okay. You sound like you're sincere. You sound downright miserable, as you should. So, what do you want me to do?"

"Ask her to take you to church. I haven't seen her there since . . . since . . ."

"You want me to ask her to take me to church? You know she doesn't have a car."

"That's right. She doesn't have a ride. I always . . ."

"Okay. I get it. I'll see if I can borrow my brother's jalopy."

Nearing Trinity Methodist the next Sunday morning, Theta began to arm herself with the disdain that'd been her lifelong escape from hurt. First, she had to be angry. Anger would open the door for Disdain.

"You know," she said to Helen, "you didn't have to drive me here. If I wanted to see him, I have every opportunity. You didn't have to come up with this charade."

Helen turned the steering wheel to pull her brother's car into the church lot. "I just want to go to church. How else will I ever see Louie? He's sure to be there."

"Okay. Plus, I refuse to stop attending a church I love just because I might run into Smiles." Saying his name hurt in a way she didn't expect. "So, thank you for driving me, for whatever reason."

Helen said, "Glad to do it. But, Theta, he does love you. He came back. He chose you."

"He didn't choose me."

"Of course he did. He's been trying to see you, but you're being stubborn."

"No, I'm being practical. He wouldn't be marrying me. He came back to marry his mother."

"*What*?"

"It's true. He came home to his mother, and his grandmother, too. He didn't come home to me. I don't want the Baby Ruth."

And there it was. Anger that would usher in defensive Disdain to save her from Disappointment just like it did as she'd watched her sisters walk away at the Louisville bus station all those years ago.

Sunday, June 23, 1946

He saw her in the church basement, sitting on a flimsy wooden folding chair. Helen was sitting beside her. Both held paper bulletins, each pretending inordinate interest as they waited for Mrs. Tom to begin playing the organ in the sanctuary overhead. Smiles was thankful they'd arrived early and were waiting with other young people for the cue to head for the stairs.

He saw that she held the bulletin like a Spanish fan, her eyes just visible above. His heart swelled. It wasn't that she was an underdog, and she certainly wasn't a kid. She had ambition. And she always knew what she wanted. She was no Grace. Or a June, whose exuberance was charmingly fun, but for him often overwhelming.

Theta was serious. Seriously everything Smiles wanted.

She saw him staring at her. He couldn't miss the deep creases appearing between her eyebrows, projecting her anger. She rolled her eyes upward, clear indication of her contempt.

And then suddenly her eyebrows rose in surprise.

Theta slowly lowered her bulletin. Junior would say her eyes were like silver dollars. Her sisters would say she'd better close her mouth before a bird flew in.

She turned her attention to Smiles, who was walking toward her with a tentative smile and pleading eyes. She smiled back, larger than he'd ever seen before.

Shining down on them both were dozens of illuminated frosted glass baskets.

Other books by

Mary Ellen Donat

Tiny Baby Girl Found in Woods: A Memoir

I'm Mary Ellen Test Suey, aka baby Rose and this is my true-life story. My friend Mary Ellen Cordell Donat, the daughter of the sheriff who investigated this case, and I will take you back to September 1955 on a cold, lonely road near Richmond, Indiana. A sweet baby girl just days old is found near the base of a tree with high weeds in the cold and eerie woods. She had been left there to die.

In the Shadow of Her Hat

In the sweltering summer of 1967 a corpse lie covered with newspapers on his living room sofa. As if the air weren't weighty with stench and flies, his widow sat a vigil beside him. *In the Shadow of Her Hat*, the story of willful America Corydon, chronicles painful life experiences beginning in her adolescence that expose and exacerbate eccentricity bordering on the madness that would lead to the shocking death bier. Over the course of five decades, America wages personal battles at home and abroad, from defying her domineering father to challenging the status quo.

Both available on Amazon as ebooks and in print.

Dear Reader: If you enjoyed this book, please leave a review on Amazon or Goodreads.

Made in the USA
Monee, IL
23 September 2021